CHRONICLES OF THE JEDI:

AN ILLUSTRATED GUIDE TO THE GALAXY'S GOLDEN AGE

CHRONICLES OF THE JEDI:

AN ILLUSTRATED GUIDE TO THE GALAXY'S GOLDEN AGE

Written by Cole Horton
Illustrated by Yihyoung Li

INSIGHT
EDITIONS

SAN RAFAEL • LOS ANGELES • LONDON

INTRODUCTION

An artist holds a special appreciation for the light, for light illuminates the artist's canvas, shines upon our subjects, and dances across landscapes. I am Jedi Master Harli Cogra, and I am so fortunate to live at a time when the light of the Force shines so brightly, and so widely across our vast galaxy. While others experience it differently, the Force speaks to me like a flowing brushstroke. It gives every life in the galaxy form, shape, and color. And in these recent years, the light shines in contrast to a growing darkness.

Some have called this the golden age of the Jedi. What follows here is my own study of these extraordinary times, looking at our history, our people, and the astonishing events that have shaped the Jedi Order. Great credit for this era of optimism must be given to Chancellor Lina Soh, whose vision of a larger, more prosperous galaxy has brought forth a series of Great Works: projects created to benefit the Republic and the Jedi's shared mission to bring light to all corners of the galaxy. The greatest of these is Starlight Beacon, a towering space station meant to serve as a shining light in one of the darkest corners of the galaxy. From this gleaming station, the Jedi have served valiantly to bring peace to the Galactic Frontier.

The prosperity and trials of today were undoubtedly shaped by the age of exploration that occurred some 150 years ago. Pathfinders and prospectors alike took to the unknown corners of the galaxy to plot new paths through hyperspace and lay the foundations for galaxy-wide communication. I recently traveled across the Outer Rim to document the breakthroughs of those brave explorers, in hopes that their understanding of hyperspace might inform the mysteries that puzzle us today.

Just over a year ago, a great disaster struck in hyperspace, setting off a chain of events that tested the Republic and the Jedi Order. Struggles against a band of raiders known as the Nihil, further complicated by battles against deadly sentient plants called the Drengir, have threatened to undo these Great Works. But in these times of burden, magnificent heroes also emerge.

I hope to share with you just some of the Jedi of our age, and their exploits, so that no matter what lies ahead, we shall all remember and appreciate their bravery and sacrifices.

Jedi Master

Harli Cogra

CHAPTER 1
FOR LIGHT AND LIFE

Unclear it is, what awaits us . . . but
reveals all, the Force does, hm?

— YODA

THE REPUBLIC AND THE JEDI

The Galactic Republic and the Jedi Order have been so long intertwined that many assume they are one entity. Indeed, these two grand bodies have a rich shared history, and the Jedi have often served the aspirations of the Republic. Some in our Order are quick to remind outsiders that the Jedi ultimately serve the Force, and the Force alone. However, that distinction is easily missed in this age of shared prosperity. The Jedi and the Republic form a symbiotic relationship. Each depends on the other to fulfill its fundamental purpose.

The Order was founded on the planet Ahch-To, far from the territory we now know as the Galactic Republic. Through the centuries, the relationship between the Jedi and the Republic ebbed and flowed, sometimes weaker and sometimes stronger. Yet as long as there has been a Republic, there has been a natural synergy between the two groups, as both seek to bring peace to a troubled and dangerous galaxy. It is no coincidence that the Republic capital of Coruscant is also the home of the Jedi Grand Temple. While some Jedi claim to want no part in politics, many have acted as negotiators at the Galactic Senate's request, or accompanied diplomatic envoys to troubled corners of the galaxy.

For a thousand generations, the Jedi have sought to ease the suffering of all beings, regardless of the dominant political regime. The Order has operated in the furthest reaches of the galaxy, be it studying the Force at remote temples, finding younglings with exceptional abilities, or promoting peace. But with Republic support, the mission of the Jedi has been realized much faster and to greater effect.

More than ever before, the Jedi share in the Republic's vision of expansion and advancement. The Pathfinders of old opened up the galaxy for the Jedi and Republic, affording us the chance to provide outreach to new systems in need. In return, the Jedi gain deeper knowledge into the galaxy and the Force. Chancellor Lina Soh, with her strong desire to achieve unity and cooperation throughout the Republic and beyond, has proven to be an especially important ally to the Jedi. Soh believes in prosperity for all galactic citizens, regardless of where they sit on the galactic map, and she advocates for a spirit of cooperation between star systems. As she seeks to widen the Republic's influence throughout the Outer Rim, she does so with the enthusiastic support of the Jedi Order, which has embraced its role in the operation of Starlight Beacon, a frontier space station we consider the peak of her Great Works.

AN ERA OF PROSPERITY

The oldest and wisest Jedi among us have begun to speak of our current age as the most successful in the history of the Republic. It is true that this era of prosperity is marked by a strong partnership between the government of the Republic and Jedi Order. However, the harmony of recent decades has also marked a closer relationship between the Jedi and the citizens of the galaxy who we have sworn to protect. Every Jedi working across the stars is helping to spread the light further than ever before.

OPPOSITE Jedi Master Stellan Gios provides sanctuary to a Gotal youngling and his grandmother in their time of need.

Our galaxy has not always been in such balance. Thankfully, our longtime enemies, the Sith, have faded from memory. Even the troubles of a century and a half ago seem far behind us. That was an age when the Republic embarked on a mission of exploration, pushing toward the frontier of the Outer Rim. Today, we all benefit from the bravery of those pioneers. Our galaxy feels larger as a consequence of Republic expansion, yet smaller thanks to the ease of travel made possible by hyperlanes. With every passing day, new systems join the Republic, Jedi temples spring up on distant worlds, and new trade lanes fuel commerce.

Communications across these great distances, while not yet perfect, have improved significantly in recent years too. The flow of information and assistance between worlds makes the galaxy safer, wiser, and stronger than ever.

All of these things bring the Jedi closer to the galaxy and its people. It is by being out *there* that we can truly live up to our mission as messengers of peace. A calm, prosperous existence is the most fertile ground for unity and goodwill to bloom. And with everything in balance, we might all find a deeper connection to the Force.

(left to right) Cibaba, Douglas Sunvale, Poreht La, Giktoo Nelmo, Lynela Kabe-Oyu, Sav Malagán, Monshi, Jorinda Boffrey, Arkoff, Tia Mirabel, and Regald Coll.

A JEDI'S PATH

Becoming a Jedi is a lifelong commitment to abiding by the light side of the Force. A Jedi will live a life full of sacrifice and selflessness, always serving others before themselves. It's also a life of mastering incredible abilities and endless learning. Above all, it is a life dictated by the will of the Force. It is by a miracle of the Force that a Jedi should find their way into the Order at all.

Jedi training begins at a very young age when a gifted child is brought to the attention of the Order. Though an emotional moment for parents, offering up a Force-sensitive child to the Jedi Order is considered a great honor to most cultures. This honor extends beyond the borders of the Republic, for even nonmember planets recognize the profound opportunity a child will have by joining the Jedi.

No journey on the Jedi's path is identical, but there are defined stages of growth, each presenting a new opportunity to learn from the Force—and the wise Jedi all around us.

JEDI YOUNGLING

The first years of a Jedi's formal training occur as a youngling, when a child is just old enough to accept instruction. Trained by a number of teachers, including those at the Grand Temple on Coruscant, younglings will be equipped with all of the basic knowledge needed to begin study of the Force. Meditation techniques, lightsaber training, Jedi philosophy, and maintaining spiritual balance are regular subjects. As they get older, a youngling will embark on a great test to earn their kyber crystal and construct their unique lightsaber. Force willing, they will carry it and all of these lessons for life.

JEDI PADAWAN

After studying for years in a temple, a youngling will be ready for the next step in their education. Padawans then become an apprentice to a Jedi Knight or Master. The two form one of the strongest bonds a Jedi can ever experience. Together, they will travel the galaxy to earn a stronger understanding of the Force, and master the skills required to be a Jedi. For adolescents, the galaxy can be full of distractions, questions, and emotions. This is a natural part of life—learning to accept and transcend those emotions is a key part of the Padawan's education. Masters often take assignments elsewhere, if they notice a strong degree of attachment between their Padawan and another. Putting distance between Padawans is usually enough to allow them to grow beyond attachment, but leaving the Order is still a choice that the apprentice can take if they're unable or unwilling to set aside their feelings.

Once their master feels they have made enough progress in these areas, a Padawan will embark on their trials to determine their readiness to become a Knight. There are no predefined trials to be taken like a test, instead it is up to the master to decide what challenge is most relevant to their apprentice. For example, Padawan Keeve Trennis passed her trials by overcoming her own self-doubt and saving a frontier planet's native population from a swarm of giant bugs.

JEDI KNIGHT

After passing the trials and participating in a knighting ceremony, a Jedi is now ready to embark without the oversight of a master to serve the Force and the Order. For some, this means being posted to one of the many temples throughout the galaxy. Others will dedicate themselves to a more specialized task like archival work, seeking out Force-sensitive younglings, or the study of the arts. Along the way, a Knight will typically be called to one of the most important tasks in the Order—taking a Padawan of their own. In their lifetime, a Jedi might take multiple Padawans in succession. In this way, the cycle continues, and the Order continues to grow.

JEDI MASTER

Those who have undertaken the most serious study and hold the deepest devotion to the Force will achieve the rank of Jedi Master. It is more than just an honorary title, for upon achieving the rank of Master, the Order expects a Jedi to forge their own path and pursue independent studies. However, some masters might still take a Padawan, or return to the Grand Temple to educate younglings. Masters are also eligible to be named to the Grand Council as leaders of the Order. For a very select few, the title of Grand Master awaits only the most illustrious among us.

Since the service of a Jedi is a lifelong commitment, the Order makes accommodations for those who are nearing the end of their path. Aging Jedi are afforded deep respect by younger members and are allowed to live out their days in relative peace, either in the comforts of the Grand Temple on Coruscant or at one of the Order's many outposts. These remote temples can offer a quieter life, far from the bustling cities of the Core.

OPPOSITE (left to right) Grand Master Lahru, Master Porter Engle, a Rodian youngling, Master Nib Assek, Knight Keeve Trennis, and Padawan Burryaga.

THE HIGH COUNCIL

The Force guides us all, but it is the Jedi High Council who helps interpret the will of the Force as leaders of the Jedi Order. The Council consists of twelve Masters who all bring a different perspective and combined centuries of experience. When significant matters must be decided, they each cast a vote to determine how the Order will act. The Council today is notable for its three Grand Masters—Yoda, Lahru, and Pra-tre Veter—who sit alongside nine other Masters to form this body of leadership.

(left to right) Yoda, Ephru Shinn, Lahru, and Pra-tre Veter.

GRAND MASTER LAHRU

Grand Master Lahru is a towering figure in the Jedi Order, both physically and in reputation. He is famous among the Jedi for his study of midi-chlorians—work that has significantly advanced our knowledge of the microscopic organisms which facilitate our connection to the Force. Now, some believe it will someday be possible to more accurately identify and measure the presence of the midi-chlorians in other life-forms. Such experience has made him a pragmatic leader and gives him an appreciation that there are rarely simple answers to the greatest questions.

GRAND MASTER PRA-TRE VETER

Pra-tre Veter has served on the Council for more than two decades and is well known for strengthening the relationship between the Jedi Council and the office of the Republic chancellor. In the wake of the Great Hyperspace Disaster, the Grand Master's travels have limited his time in the Jedi temple, as he has taken on additional duties in the absence of Grand Master Yoda.

GRAND MASTER YODA

Master Yoda's service to the Order is as legendary as it is lengthy. Yoda has been a Jedi for more than six centuries and shows no sign of slowing. There is seemingly not a Jedi in the Order who doesn't know who he is. Jedi often tell stories of their encounters with the Grand Master, who is prone to imparting lifelong wisdom to younglings. In recent years, Yoda has taken an interest in the hands-on education of Padawans, choosing to take a sabbatical from the Council to serve as an instructor on a training vessel, the *Star Hopper*. In his absence, Master Ephru Shinn holds his seat

as a temporary replacement. The Mon Calamari Jedi believes that the role of the Order is to be a symbol of peace, and she does not let her temporary status stop her from voicing her beliefs. She is cautious when considering taking actions that might lead to violence, even when facing threats such as the Nihil.

ADA-LI CARRO

Master Carro is a Jedi with a special eye for architecture, lending her expertise to the expansion of temple outposts across the galaxy. She effectively created the blueprint for modern temples, incorporating classical designs with modern technologies, and pioneered the techniques we now use to refit and restore older locations. Her work building across the galaxy was recognized and rewarded with a seat on the High Council.

KEATON MURAG

The human Keaton Murag was elevated to the High Council just prior to the Great Disaster. Prior to returning to Coruscant, he served as the marshal of the Naboo temple. While there, he earned the respect of the Naboo monarchy for saving hundreds of lives during a mining accident. He was quick to downplay his bravery, but accounts from survivors suggest that he single-handedly used the Force to hold back a terrible explosion as the miners escaped.

OPPO RANCISIS

Master Rancisis is a renowned strategist and vocal proponent of temple outposts. The Thisspiasian Jedi is familiar with the frontier, given his time overseeing construction of the Jedi temple on Falaston, which, at the time, was the most remote temple in operation. Decades later, he has returned to Coruscant to serve on the Council, but his experience in the Outer Rim proves valuable when the Council weighs issues concerning expansion.

YARAEL POOF

Though he is an expert practitioner of Jedi mind-tricks and illusions, Master Yarael Poof rarely needs them during his many diplomatic missions. This perceptive negotiator and skilled teacher was called on by Chancellor Soh to investigate the cause of the Great Hyperspace Disaster. He led the investigation into the *Legacy Run* incident with an eye to prevent future Emergences.

RANA KANT

The Duros Master Rana Kant earned her seat on the Council many times over, though she originally turned down the offer more than once. Kant preferred to serve outside of the Council chambers, where she could more closely assist galactic citizens. Earlier in her career, Kant escorted pilgrims to the planet Castell, which proved to be a deeply influential experience. As a result, Kant believed that the most essential Jedi virtues could only come from traveling the galaxy. Even in her later years, she rebuked any ideas for retirement, choosing to remain active until her final days. Master Kant became one with the Force due to natural causes shortly after the Great Disaster, and her seat on the Council was filled by her former Padawan, Master Stellan Gios.

TERI ROSASON

Council member Teri Rosason is a shrewd negotiator, who is regularly called on to oversee critical relationships. Though diplomatic outside of the Order, Rosason is at times combative, and she was especially critical of Avar Kriss's handling of the Drengir infestation. She disapproved of the latitude afforded to the marshal in hunting the threat, believing that outpost Jedi should consult with the Council more regularly before engaging in prolonged missions, particularly combat actions that might fall outside the Jedi's stated goals of preserving peace.

ABOVE (left to right) Keaton Murag, Oppo Rancisis, and Ada-Li Carro.

SOLEIL AGRA

The Nautolan Master Soleil Agra is a fine pilot and expert at bridging minds through the Force. She pushed the Order forward in its understanding of Drift formation flying, likening the experience to a school of fish on her native planet of Glee Anselm. Her compassion and quiet strength are inspiring in the wake of recent tragedies, especially for Padawans and Knights who struggle to come to terms with what they have experienced.

GRAND MASTER RY KI-SAKKA

The human Ry Ki-Sakka replaced Master Jora Malli on the High Council after her fall during the Battle of Kur. His new posting required him to return to Coruscant after spending most of his life in the far reaches of the galaxy. Elder Jedi say that Master Ki-Sakka is a living example of the old Pathfinder spirit—he learned to operate far from the Republic's traditional borders and, as a result, values self-sufficiency.

ADAMPO

Master Adampo is among the most studious of the High Council, and a favorite among the Order's many archivists. The Yarkoran is a noted linguist who speaks a variety of languages, both living and extinct. Some claim that he is fluent in more forgotten tongues than some droids will ever learn. Adampo strongly supported Chancellor Lina Soh's efforts to build science vessels for research in the Outer Rim and was a proponent of expanding the archives in outpost temples, but he was among those on the Council who shied away from any conflict. However, as the events of the Great Disaster unfolded, it became clear to Adampo that peace was no longer an option when facing the Nihil.

THE GRAND TEMPLE

At the center of the Galactic Republic is the very heart of the Jedi Order, the Grand Temple on Coruscant. As one of the most enduring icons of our Order, this is the home of the High Council. The entire surface of Coruscant is covered in one giant city, and the temple stands thousands of levels above the planet's now-lost surface. At its highest point, a temple spire plays host to Council meetings where Jedi leaders consider and debate issues that could determine the fate of the galaxy. Coruscant is also the home of the Galactic Senate, giving the Grand Temple both a physical and symbolic connection to the Republic for which the Jedi protect.

OPPOSITE (left to right) Soleil Agra, Ry Ki-Sakka, and Adampo.
ABOVE (left to right) Rana Kant, Teri Rosason, and Yarael Poof.

The Grand Temple affords both visiting and resident Jedi the finest resources. Those looking to study can find the most complete archive in the galaxy. For more senior members, the archive's vaults hold treasured relics including holocrons detailing the Order's most obscure knowledge.

For those interested in history and art, the temple is home to the largest and most complete collection of statues, tapestries, reliefs, and mosaics collected for centuries by Jedi travelers. It's common to see a clan of younglings standing before each stunning piece of art, assigned by their masters to look for the deeper meaning each piece holds.

Jedi seeking to meditate might be surprised to find serenity among the bustle of Coruscant's planet-city, but they will find great peace in the meditation halls of the Grand Temple. More advanced meditation techniques are also encouraged here, including a walk across the Kyber Arch. It stands within one of the temple's largest meditation chambers and was constructed with thousands of tiny kyber crystals. Each was retrieved from the lightsaber of a Jedi fallen in battle. The radiant arch sparkles in the light, beckoning Jedi to attempt crossing from one side to the other. At its midpoint, the arch is incredibly narrow, symbolizing the perils that fallen Jedi faced.

Yet, trappings and material things are not what really make the Grand Temple so impressive. The Force strongly flows here, and the entire Order benefits from having a connection to this extraordinary place. Some visiting Jedi believe the Force can be heard more clearly here, allowing for more peaceful meditation and clarity when interpreting the will of the Force. It is no coincidence that such a prominent site should be located at its exact spot, as there have been important religious structures at this location since antiquity. The temple is built upon layers of history—including that of an ancient Sith shrine—making it far more significant than many realize.

FORGING A DEEPER CONNECTION

Throughout this hallowed age of peace and prosperity, the Jedi Order has been afforded a rare opportunity to deepen our understanding of ourselves, the galaxy, and the Force itself. Amid the conflict and strife of centuries past, there was little opportunity for the Jedi to be so reflective. Worse yet, these distractions meant that great knowledge was lost or destroyed by our enemies, the Sith. Their menace has been gone for centuries, and the Republic is more stable than it has been in hundreds of years. It could be argued that in modern times our connection to the Force is stronger than it has ever been.

Jedi scholars in recent times have expanded our understanding of the Force. For instance, scholars of our time have made great breakthroughs in engineering by using the Force to analyze raw materials.

When a Jedi's connection to the Force becomes unstable, there are multiple avenues to restore their sacred link, and recenter themselves after difficult missions. Jedi counselors are specially trained to help others work through traumatic events when individual meditation is not enough. Additionally, we have advanced our knowledge of foundational Jedi techniques used to restore spiritual balance when we veer too closely to the dark side of the Force.

In the past century and a half, some have even taken more extreme measures to forge a deeper connection. The Barash Vow, named after Jedi Knight Barash Silvain more than a century ago, is an extreme commitment—the ultimate communion with the Force, which requires a Jedi to spend years in contemplative meditation. Some choose this path after making a severe mistake, while others choose to take the vow after losing their connection with the Force.

Then there are the Wayseekers, Jedi who choose to remain committed to the Order's teachings but break from its oversight. They follow the Force and the Force alone, allowing their connection to the cosmic energy to tell them where to go next. The path of the Wayseeker requires a deep trust in the Force and one's own abilities but can lead to a life of fulfillment nonetheless.

The very nature of the Force is experienced differently by individual Jedi. When focusing their powers, a Jedi will visualize the Force in their own way. Some, like Avar Kriss, hear the Force like a song, with the Force of others comprising distinct notes. Master Loden Greatstorm visualized the Force as a gusting wind, while Master Estala Maru sees the Force as window lights in an endlessly sprawling nighttime city. The Wookiee Padawan Burryaga sees the Force as a single leaf upon a towering tree from his home planet of Kashyyyk. Others, like Elzar Mann and Vernestra Rwoh, associate the Force with water. Mann sees it as an endless storm-tossed sea, its depths and secrets waiting to be explored. On the other hand, Rwoh visualizes a steady stream.

Elder Jedi often say that there is much to be learned about a person by the way they see the Force. It is a reflection of who they are, both their greatest strengths and their most difficult deficiencies. But we Jedi do not decide how the Force speaks to us. We can only listen, and watch. With great focus, we might just find what the Force wants us to see.

OPPOSITE TOP LEFT Coruscant.

ABOVE Barash Silvain forges a deep connection with the Force.

Padawan Burryaga visualizes the Force as a great tree on Kashyyyk.

Elzar Mann envisions a stormy sea, fitting for his often-tempestuous connection to the Force.

THE GALACTIC MAP

The galactic map is far different than it was just a century and a half ago. In those times, Republic territory was centered around its long-standing territories in the Core and Mid Rim. Systems in the Mid Rim were considered distant, while travel to the further reaches of the galaxy was an arduous undertaking.

The Great Hyperspace Rush changed all of that. New, faster, and safer routes to the Outer Rim reshaped how we see the galaxy. While the Republic is still most powerful in the core regions of this expanse, the explorers of a century ago have paved the way for expansion today. With every passing cycle, more worlds join the Republic, and more Jedi temples are constructed to spread the light of our Order. We are all the Republic, and this map illustrates both how far we have come and how far we still have to go.

Yet on the furthest reaches of the frontier, a band of raiders known as the Nihil operate without regard for peace and order. Through devastating raids, the Nihil now control the edges of the Outer Rim.

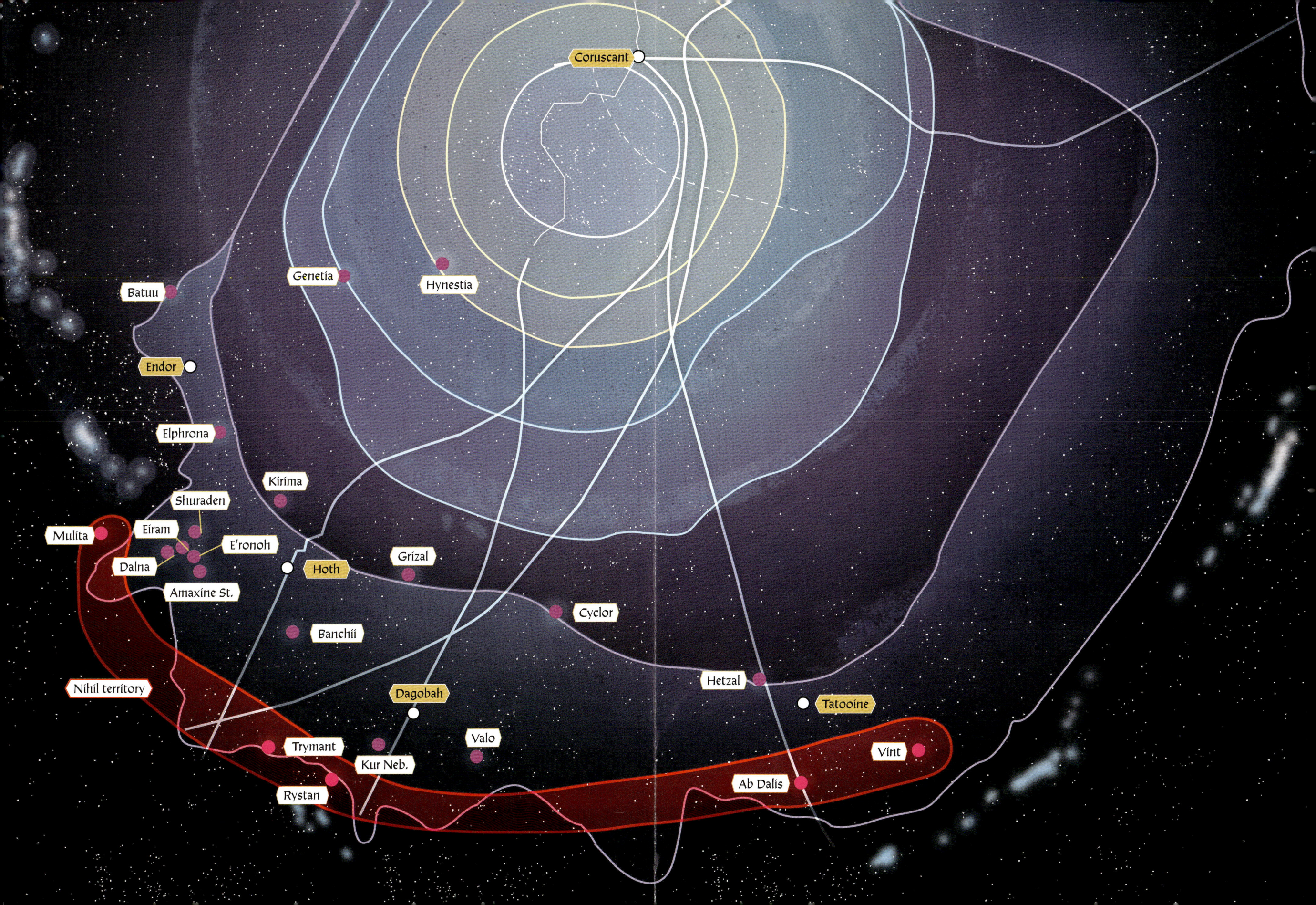

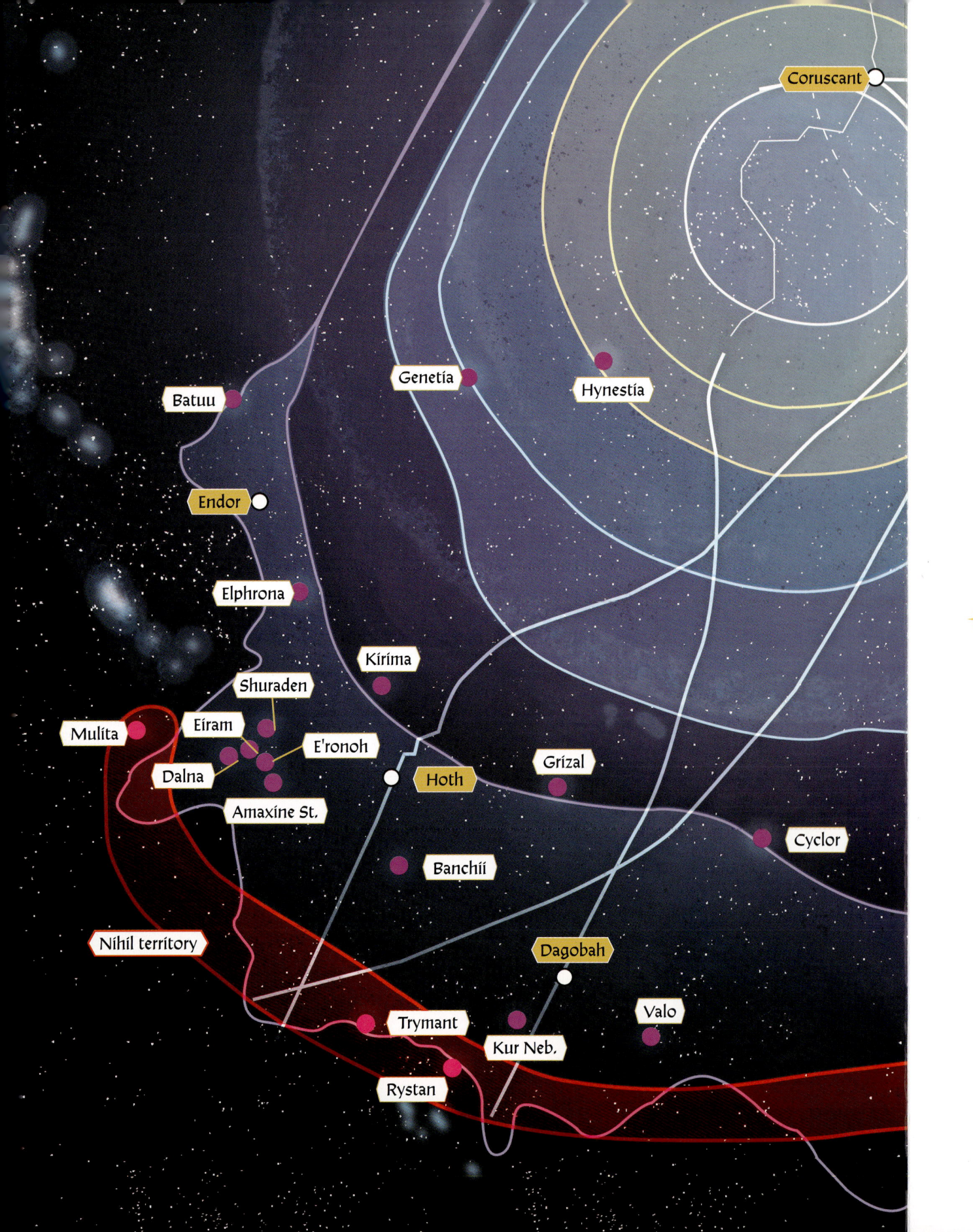

HYPERSPACE: THEORY, PHILOSOPHY, AND HISTORY

Hyperspace. Light speed. The Paths. There are many ways to describe how a starship travels vast distances through the galaxy, and even more theories as to how it works. Thanks to advances in hyperdrive technology, the charting of well-trodden hyperspace lanes, and the widespread installation of hyperdrives in most crewed vessels, travelers today take the ability to fly faster than light for granted. But it was not always so simple, and we still do not have all the answers to this miracle of modern space travel.

The discovery of hyperspace travel has been the key to galactic civilization as we know it. In fact, a government like the Republic spread across vast parsecs of the galaxy would be near impossible without the ability to travel great distances so quickly. Similarly, the Jedi Order would not be able to build its ranks, or explore the vast mysteries of the Force, had it not been for the advent of hyperdrives.

Despite the fact that the Order teaches countless hours of hyperspace theory to its Padawans, there is still much that experts don't know. There are some Jedi philosophers who believe that hyperspace, being part of all that surrounds us, can be seen and sensed through the cosmic Force. They see it as lanes or rivers of energy that spring forth from some unknown origin. They say that we are simply passengers upon those streams, following each one to where they flow, but ultimately, their beginning and end points are determined by the Force. Others believe hyperspace is another dimension, a sort of shadow of the world where we live.

Outside the Order, spacers and prospectors endlessly debate their own theories, some scientific, and some downright fanciful. One might claim hyperspace to be navigable wormholes. Others believe that they are routes carved out by an ancient race of spacefarers that no longer exists. The more educated experts generally agree that each hyperspace lane is its own distinct plane of existence. Ships with a hyperdrive make the jump into this alternate dimension, and by following a well-explored path, they voyage more quickly and more safely than realspace travel.

HYPERSPACE PROSPECTING

Where there is danger, there is the promise of profit, and hyperspace prospecting offered plenty of both. At its simplest, the job of a hyperspace prospector is to discover and plot safe routes through the dangerous galaxy. Knowledge of these routes could be sold to the highest bidder. Private interests could also control the routes, looking to collect tolls for its usage. The safer and faster the route, the more credits there were to be had.

A profession largely dedicated to exploring the vastness of space, a prospector's life was full of danger and unknowns. Spacefarers faced black holes, asteroid belts, gravity fields, supernovas, imploded stars, pods of giant creatures called purrgil, and more. But the greatest threat was rarely external—more often than not, it was the prospector's own mind. Whether it was the paralyzing solitude, or some mysterious side effect of jumping in and out of hyperspace, madness always threatened to creep in on a lonely prospector drifting through space.

Prospecting was not only lucrative for those finding new routes—whole industries grew around the business of exploration. Companies like that of the San Tekka clan would pay settlers to build lives on faraway planets, advertising handsome rewards for living there and establishing local infrastructure. If a location became an important outpost, the rewards could be life changing. The settlers who took the leap often had nothing to lose but their lives.

Those who profited most were the families at the heads of the now-famous corporations. More than a century after the rush, the Grafs remain famously wealthy and have diversified their business into shipping and financing interests that stretch galaxy-wide.

After the initial rush had slowed, the San Tekkas became the next prominent family to find a fortune in the prospecting business. The San Tekka clan had been prospectors for some time but were never counted among the great families. They were, at best, hardscrabble fortune-seekers. That is, until they suddenly found a streak of seemingly unexplainable luck, eventually finding fame for mapping high-value routes. But at the height of their success, a great tragedy came. Mari, a young daughter of the San Tekkas, was kidnapped, and the San Tekkas never saw her again. It is said that the family never fully recovered from the loss of Mari, even after the one hundred years that have passed since.

Time has enshrined the prospectors into legend, but many often forget that for every

OPPOSITE Hyperspace prospectors like "Sunshine" Dobbs are a hardy, brave folk.

successful prospector, there were many more who never found a single route, or worse, never returned from their travels. The Great Rush has ended, and countless ships pass through the spacelanes without even considering how they got there.

What was once a dangerous and daring profession has even taken a new name. Now, prospectors prefer to call themselves "hyperspace surveyors" to sound more respectable. Over the decades, the most well-equipped explorers developed proprietary algorithms to predict the most likely routes and employed teams of navulators, or hyperlane experts, to analyze the data. The Great Rush might be over, and the life of a prospector has changed, but hyperspace travel remains big business.

PATHFINDER TEAMS

More than a century and a half ago, the pursuit of knowledge led Jedi to partner with the Republic in a great age of exploration. Leading these quests were brave teams of Pathfinders, both Jedi and non-Jedi alike, who were otherwise known as Outer Rim Exploration Teams. These teams struck out to new parts of the Outer Rim to lay a groundwork for expansion. Working closely with comms teams and EX droids, pilots, medics, and droids were enlisted to form small Pathfinder teams, whose remote missions appealed to those with a strong yearning for adventure.

Joining each of the Republic's Pathfinder teams were usually two Jedi—a Knight and a Padawan—to provide aid wherever needed. A Jedi's skills were invaluable when stitching together hyperlanes, or planting the first lines of communication in remote areas. Further prospecting or communications teams would follow, but these Pathfinders were on the leading edge of the expansion efforts. That also meant that the Pathfinder Jedi were the first to render aid to any local populations in need. It was this mission of mercy that appealed to the Jedi Council when they agreed to lend members of the Order to the Pathfinder effort.

BELOW (left to right) Master Helion Voss, Padawan Benj Marko, pilot Sallee Ooph, medic Grint Rupar, a communications droid, communications specialist Lirah Danch, astromech droid GT-22, and communications specialist Rol Egry.

OPPOSITE Pathfinder vessels bring aid to frontier planets in need and lay the foundations for intergalactic communication. The sturdy engineering of these ships is essential, as Pathfinders also search for new hyperlanes.

Today, we live with reminders of the age of exploration all around us. Hyperspace buoys and communications lines established more than a century ago are sometimes still in active use. Star systems that were then newly discovered are now thriving members of the Republic. A fine example of this is Hetzal—once far removed from the Republic, today its fertile soils have been transformed by Republic progress. Hetzal has burgeoned into one of the most productive agricultural worlds in the galaxy. As a planet that is vital to the production of bacta, a healing drug with the potential to help many in the galaxy, we all benefit from the advances in medicinal agronomy pioneered by Hetzal's people.

Yet despite these successes, not all expeditions ended positively. When the Republic first ventured into Togruta space, the initial interactions ended poorly. As a result of those early confrontations, tensions existed for some 150 years and have only recently been improved thanks to the outreach of Chancellor Lina Soh.

THE FRONTIER JEDI

Almost two centuries ago, the Jedi of the frontier gave up a life among comfortable temples in the Core for a life on the fringes of the galaxy. Only a relative few took to the frontier in those days, and they were far outnumbered by those Jedi who never strayed from the Republic. Any Jedi might sometimes encounter risks and unknowns, but the life of a Pathfinder meant uncertainty and danger at almost every turn. Old-timers still debate what was more dangerous: charting a new hyperlane or discovering what waited on the other side.

Jedi on the frontier had to prepare for all situations and be willing to face them without the assistance of the Order at large. The remote nature of the frontier often meant that a Jedi was completely alone, and could rely only upon themselves or their small Pathfinder team. A good Pathfinder was equal parts explorer, engineer, diplomat, doctor, and warrior. Frontier Jedi were resilient, self-sufficient types who often returned from their time in the Outer Rim hardened and grizzled by the experience.

Whether for their bravery in battle or their kindness helping those in need, many great heroes emerged from this period. We remember Rok Buran, the legendary survivalist with a renowned connection to the natural world. Some of the most memorable tales of this age center the legendary Jedi Knight Barnabas Vim, whose theological studies sent him on quests throughout the frontier.

A century and a half ago, the Jedi also worked to promote peace in the outlying regions. The long-standing war between Eiram and E'ronoh might still be raging had it not been for negotiations led by the Jedi, including Masters Char-Ryl-Roy and Creighton Sun. When trouble came to Jedha, Jedi like Vildar Mac earned their place in the galactic

(left to right) Vildar Mac, Mattea Cathley, Rok Buran, Zallah Macri, Barnabas Vim, Char-Ryl-Roy, Sarra Venalskar, Creighton Sun, Lee Harrow.

history books. Temple outpost training still recalls the example set by Zallah Macri who laid down a fine standard of leadership in her days on Port Haileap. Yet, she is also an example of the dangers faced in the frontier. Master Zallah and her Padawan went missing from their post, never to be seen alive again.

FOLLOWERS OF THE FORCE

The Force surrounds and penetrates all of us, binding the galaxy together, so it is no surprise that the Jedi are not the only ones who share a connection to it. In fact, there are thousands of different interpretations and names for this cosmic energy. There are nearly as many groups who coalesce around it, study it, and revere it. And even though the Force belongs to all beings, there are those who fear and control it.

Some of these religious groups share similar values to the Jedi Order. The Guardians of the Whills are counted among the groups who seek peace and enlightenment through the Force. The guardians dedicate themselves to protecting the Temple of the Kyber on the moon of Jedha, though they are not Force-users themselves.

Though its members do not have the ability to control or manipulate the mystical energy field, the Church of the Force is a devout group growing in popularity among pockets across the galaxy. For example, the church has gained a surprising foothold on Naboo, even among some of its most prominent houses.

Some hold strong convictions about the Force, and how it should be used. Though they have faded from most memories, the Path of the Open Hand once believed that no living being should attempt to use or control the Force. They had deep respect for it, so much so that they believed no one was worthy of its miracles. Less extreme displays of spirituality exist among members of the Brotherhood of the Beatific Countenance who take a vow of silence so far as to conceal any piece of their own self-expression.

Long ago the Jedi came into conflict with the Sith, an offshoot of our own Order who twisted our teachings in a bid to use the Force for their own power. They embraced the dark side of the Force, tapping into their own fear or anger to unlock unnatural abilities. The Sith were defeated centuries ago, but they are not the only ones to have a connection to the dark side of the Force. The Yellow Fellowship established shrines long ago that are still rumored to hold dark energies within their stone walls. The fellowship died out long ago, and much of what we know about them today comes from their ruins and artifacts.

BELOW Members of the Path of the Open Hand including The Mother (center) and The Herald (right).

THE EIRAM-E'RONOH CONFLICT: THE FOREVER WAR

When the Republic embarked on its mission of exploration, it found a corner of the galaxy that had been troubled by war for many years. Conflict between two neighboring worlds, Eiram and E'ronoh, was born from a standoff over their system's hyperspace gateway—a point of access that would allow safe and profitable trade along a route that embarked from the Eiram system. This conflict had begun to spill over into nearby systems when the Republic arrived. The five years of fighting saw the conflict become known as the Forever War, which invited lawlessness, deep factional divides, and led to great suffering as shortages threatened to starve the nearby worlds of food and fuel. The Jedi negotiated a peace between Eiram and E'ronoh, but the accord simply pushed the conflict out of sight. While open war between them ended, a new phase of proxy battles and political maneuvering began.

While the Republic was never formally drawn into the combat, the government and the Jedi were caught up in the affair. At the time, two chancellors governed the Republic—Chancellors Greylark and Mollo. However, scandal brought an end to the dual chancellorship experiment: Chancellor Greylark's son secretly worked to extend the war, a discovery that rocked the political world and relations with the frontier alike. For the Jedi's part, they had hoped to avoid fighting, but the defenders of light could not stand idly by as innocent lives were threatened.

Distrust between the two planets continued for more than a century. It was some twenty-five years ago that the two planets' proxy war left them exposed to a criminal plot. The queen regent of Eiram and the monarch of E'ronoh were kidnapped by a gang known as the Directorate who hoped to stoke conflict once again, in the hopes of destabilizing the government, thus making room for criminal syndicates to take power. The Jedi mounted a rescue effort to prevent a new war from erupting, eventually allowing the Republic to earn the trust of Eiram's queens. After more than a century of fighting and resentment, Eiram put aside its conflict with neighboring E'ronoh and eventually decided to join the Republic.

THE BATTLE OF JEDHA

After five years of war in the Eiram system, the Jedi attempted to broker a peace agreement between Eiram and its neighbors on E'ronoh. They arranged for the peace treaty to be signed on a neutral site, the moon of Jedha. There, the Convocation of the Force, a council of Force religions representing different organizations, held court among Jedha's sacred sites. All hoped that peace could be found under the watchful eye of these Force religions, but instead a battle erupted that forever changed perceptions on the usage of the Force.

An extremist group who believed no one should use the Force, the Path of the Open Hand, interrupted the signing of the treaty. The battle that ensued brought down one of Jedha's ancient sandstone statues and laid waste to parts of the holy city. The Jedi fought valiantly to restore order, but the damage was done. The Battle of Jedha broke the cease-fire between Eiram and E'ronoh, reigniting the Forever War.

OPPOSITE An ancient Jedi statue falls during the Battle of Jedha.

Today, Jedha remains a holy place, but the multitude of Force religions no longer hold council there. The Guardians of the Whills continue to keep the peace to ensure pilgrims may visit undisturbed, but the Jedi no longer have a permanent presence in that sacred place.

PORTER ENGLE AND BARASH SILVAIN

Even though Porter Engle and Barash Silvain were akin to siblings, they were opposites in so many ways. Where Porter was terse and undiplomatic, Barash was outgoing. Even in dress, Porter's dark robes stood in contrast to the radiant white worn by Barash. The two were accepted into the Jedi Order, where they achieved the rank of Knight. A century and a half ago, the Force led them to the planet Bardotta, and it was there that their paths truly diverged.

Bardotta was under siege by pirates and mercenaries. Cornered by hundreds of enemies, Jedi Porter attempted to warn the marauders not to attack, but his pleas went unheeded. Porter Engle was left with no choice but to take lives in order to free the planet. Using his saber, Porter miraculously deflected shot after shot fired by the mercenaries. It was a display of skill so magnificent that it earned him the title, Blade of Bardotta. His legendary exploits that day continue to be revered more than a century later. Even in retirement, Porter Engle is a legend among the Jedi for his heroic deeds. At some three hundred years old, Porter fought valiantly at the Battle of Valo against the Nihil.

His "sister" Barash was not so fortunate. Jedi Barash entered the fray at Bardotta believing she could help the people of that planet, but her plan was miscalculated and many died as a result.

Porter Engle in combat on Bardotta.

Distraught by her failure, Barash Silvain took to a self-imposed exile to reconsider her actions and her connection to the Force. This exile was her legacy, and taking on such severe seclusion is today known as taking the Barash Vow.

FRONTIER TEMPLES

As the Jedi worked to expand the light of the Force across the galaxy, the Order established new temple outposts across the frontier to serve as a permanent shelter for its members. In centuries past, early temples were often located near a Force nexus, a location with an unusually high concentration of the Force flowing through it. As the Jedi Order evolved over the millennia, temples on these sites were built and rebuilt, lost and rediscovered as time marched on. Some served as way stations for Jedi bringing younglings to the Order from the frontier. These were vital stopping-off points for Jedi traveling at a time when hyperlanes were not clearly established.

There was a time when Falaston was home to one of the most remote Jedi temples, but in working with the Republic, the Jedi have since pushed even further into the frontier. The older generation of temples established in the wake of the Great Hyperspace Rush were often renovated and improved more than a century later during the expansion of the Republic under Chancellor Lina Soh.

Because they are built using native materials and incorporate local nuances into their designs, no two temples are alike. They mix local architecture with many of the trappings of the Grand Temple on Coruscant, sharing common features such as meditation chambers, peaceful gardens, and sunlit passageways. Most house a modest archive offering a small slice of Jedi knowledge far from the main archive on Coruscant. They also serve as a communications network to relay messages or accept distress signals from nearby systems.

All of these features were in service to the Order's mission on these remote worlds. In part, they served as a refuge for frontier Jedi to reconnect to the Force and recuperate from whatever mission drew them to these far reaches. Perhaps most importantly, they existed to serve the nearby populations. Locals could call upon the Jedi for assistance when facing natural disasters, trouble with local predators, or other challenges that vex local peacekeepers. In some of the more remote outposts, there was no local law enforcement, and the Jedi did their best to maintain peace among the scattered residents. Bandits, pirates, smugglers, and organized crime were staples of the Outer Rim, so the Jedi did their best to deter such troubles. When violence did occur, the proximity of a temple allowed the Jedi to respond much more quickly than if a call was answered from the Core.

It is said that a seedling cannot grow to its full potential in the shadow of a great tree. Similarly, a Padawan cannot truly prosper if they don't leave the Grand Temple on Coruscant. As the number of temples grew, being "outposted" became a common step in a Padawan's training where even a temporary assignment far from the Core gave an apprentice valuable perspective on the galaxy and its inhabitants. With so few Jedi assigned to these outposts, a Padawan could count on plenty of hands-on experience. Locals rarely understood the difference between a Padawan and a Knight, and thus had no hesitation asking younger members to play a visible role in assisting with their troubles.

OPPOSITE Jedi Outpost on Elphrona.

CHAPTER 3
BEACONS OF THE REPUBLIC

Starlight is a symbol of hope for the entire galaxy,
a symbol of trust, of unity. Whenever you feel
alone . . . Whenever darkness closes in . . . hear
our signal and know that the Force is with you.
Know that we are with you. This is our promise.
This is our covenant. For light and life.

— AVAR KRISS

STARLIGHT BEACON

Republic Chancellor Lina Soh's mission to bring the light of the Republic to the Outer Rim was meant to be enabled by the pinnacle of her Great Works—a series of state-of-the-art space stations known as beacons. The first, and the only one to be completed, was appropriately named Starlight, as it was envisioned to be the first of such stations constructed to bring greater prosperity to the frontier. Starlight Beacon was the first ray of hope for many systems in this distant part of the galaxy. The station was designed to broadcast a signal, a reassuring chime, that anyone with even the most rudimentary equipment could hear for hundreds of parsecs around the station. The sound would help everyone find their way.

Having been designed by the renowned Jedi architect Palo Hidalla, specialists and engineers from across the Republic flocked to the new project, their work supervised by the famously meticulous Shai Tennem. His eye for detail met its match with the fabled craftsmanship of the Riosa workers who constructed the bulk of the station.

The Jedi Council lent more than just their support for this effort, as Starlight Beacon was akin to a mobile, space-worthy Jedi temple. From that gleaming station, the Jedi worked hand in hand with the Republic to operate it and provide security. Starlight featured its own Jedi Quarter from which the Padawans, Knights, and Masters who were stationed there might find a home among the stars. For many, a posting to Starlight Beacon was a great honor, rivaling postings at the Grand Temple on Coruscant.

Many Jedi—either posted to Starlight Beacon or just passing through—found a quiet spot for

meditation among the station's bio-gardens. Each biosphere zone welcomed visitors to walk through re-creations of various worlds in the Outer Rim Territories. The most impressive of these gardens featured spiraling walkways that arched over soils imported from the Outer Rim. This ground was so fertile that it could support a three-hundred-meter-tall tree reaching nearly to the top of the transparisteel dome that covered the garden.

The Nihil and Drengir threat made the Starlight Beacon security tower one of the busiest hubs on the entire station. Processing prisoners was an unexpectedly common duty, requiring Republic or Jedi peacekeepers to interrogate and log each captured Nihil before they were sent off station for reform.

To support the Republic's mission of greater prosperity, a merchant's tower brought traders together, each with a variety of wares. Starlight's docking bay was a flurry of activity, as ships of every type came to find food, fuel, and new

ABOVE Starlight Beacon's numerous garden modules welcome meditation.

OPPOSITE ABOVE Jedi launch bay.

OPPOSITE BELOW Starlight's glimmering passageways.

Debris of the *Legacy Run* threatens Hetzal Prime.

opportunities. The Republic's arrival to this corner of the Outer Rim caused a flurry of activity as traders packed transports to the brim to move goods before taxes might be imposed. However, many simply sought a safe refuge to rest, and those looking for a break could grab a drink in a quiet tap bar named Unity, a welcoming den for those who seek a respite from the bustling grandeur found elsewhere.

THE GREAT HYPERSPACE DISASTER

Republic expansion into the Outer Rim was a signal to the galaxy that a new age of prosperity had begun. As the Republic prepared for the official dedication of its new Starlight Beacon, the Jedi constructed new temples. Meanwhile, citizens of the Republic sought to stake their claim on the newly added member worlds.

Among the many ships making the journey to the frontier was an aging freighter operated by the Byne Guild, the *Legacy Run*. Loaded to capacity with cargo and passengers seeking a better life, the *Legacy Run* traveled on one of the most well-mapped routes in the Outer Rim. It was captained by a veteran of both military and civilian flight, Hedda Casset. Hands-on in the best sense, she kept her vessel in peak condition, and her crew in top form. There was no indication that the *Legacy Run* was going to depart for the Outer Rim and never return.

While traveling through hyperspace, Captain Casset was forced to make a sudden evasive maneuver. The ship avoided the obstacle in its path, which we now know to be a Nihil ship, but the strenuous maneuver was too much for the *Legacy Run*'s aging frame to withstand. The freighter disintegrated in mid-flight. Parts of the ship were instantly destroyed, while others broke away and continued flying uncontrollably through hyperspace for some time—a great threat to any planets in the way. When exiting hyperspace, the debris of the *Legacy Run* turned into a high-speed molten projectile as dangerous as a large meteorite. The fragments could tear through ships and destroy entire cities that lay in their path. The tragedy for those on board the *Legacy Run* soon turned into an impending disaster for planets throughout the Outer Rim. The Great Disaster had begun.

For a time, even the most learned experts could not explain how it happened. Yet, the impossible was possible. A ship had collided with another object in hyperspace. Fragments of the *Legacy Run* were exiting hyperspace throughout the Outer Rim. Millions were in peril and the safest lanes were unstable. Hyperspace was experiencing a sickness, and it was up to the Jedi to find a cure.

OPPOSITE Padawan Bell Zettifar and his Master, Loden Greatstorm defend the citizens of Hetzal.

THE JEDI AT HETZAL

When fragments of the *Legacy Run* exited hyperspace, it sent deadly wreckage flying through realspace at terminal velocities. The first system threatened was Hetzal, a prosperous Outer Rim farming center that is home to millions of beings.

The system's most populous planet, Hetzal Prime, dedicated nearly all of its available space, including buildings and the planet's oceans, to agricultural production. Hetzal was more than just a thriving food-growing hub for this part of the galaxy—it was on the forefront of cultivating the ingredients for bacta, an emerging therapy

that had already shown great promise as a medical remedy. The agricultural scientists in this system were working to perfect mass production, a would-be breakthrough that would benefit the entire Republic. But when fragments of the *Legacy Run* emerged in the system, that progress was under threat. The Hetzal system only had enough ships to save a small fraction of its forty billion inhabitants, and so, a system-wide evacuation began.

Just when all hope seemed lost, a glimmer of hope appeared on their sensors. It was the Jedi. Help was on the way.

The Jedi arrived with little more than an hour to act before a cataclysm. Their ship, the *Third Horizon*, radiated with hope. As if by the will of the Force, the ship and its complement of Jedi had been delayed leaving Starlight Beacon and had been passing nearby the Hetzal system when the Great Disaster struck. Had their departure happened on schedule, there would have been no one close enough to provide assistance to the beings of Hetzal. But by this miracle, they came.

The gleaming *Third Horizon* was part of the Republic's small defense fleet. From its bridge, the Jedi Master Avar Kriss stood by to coordinate the Jedi and their Republic allies, including nearly thirty Republic Longbeams and more than fifty Jedi Vectors who raced across the system. Deep in meditation, Avar Kriss's gifted ability to connect with other Jedi through the Force undoubtedly saved billions of lives. There was no time to plan the rescue effort, but by bridging the Jedi's minds, Master Avar was able to monitor the situation in real time and reposition her fellow Jedi in response.

Guided by the Force, and connected through the song of Avar Kriss, each Jedi set off to different corners of the system with the same simple

conviction: help. Some flew their Vectors to clear debris before it struck, or escort the surge of vessels attempting to navigate out of the system. Others raced to the surface of Hetzal Prime and its nearby Fruited Moon to evacuate survivors. Chaos and fear among the desperate population threatened to cloud the judgment of the Jedi, but through intense focus and determination, each found a way to be the heroes the galaxy needed. The light of the Jedi Order shone bright that day, but soon an even darker shadow threatened to undo all the good that had been done. A cataclysmic event threatened to destroy the entire system if the Jedi could not find a way to avert the disaster.

THE SONG OF THE FORCE

A Jedi's strength is the Force, and the Force binds the galaxy together. But who is to bind the Jedi? That falls to a rare set of individuals such as Avar Kriss. Master Kriss has a rare skill to detect the bonds between Force-users, and strengthen the connections between them. This talent allows her to recognize distant sensations and locations, though to her, this is all perceived through a musical harmony. Her "Song of the Force" was crucial to the Jedi rescue effort at Hetzal.

The Jedi worked admirably to rescue survivors that day. Most fragments had been diverted, or the threatened population evacuated in time, but the final piece of the *Legacy Run* proved to be the most dangerous. Among the ship's cargo was a tank of liquid Tibanna gas that had somehow survived intact. The container was on course to

OPPOSITE Avar Kriss connects Jedi on Hetzal and abroad through the Song of the Force.

strike the system's largest sun, threatening to cause an extraordinary chain reaction that would destroy everything in the system. Dozens of Jedi across the system stood their ground, and through the Force, they found a way.

The plan was simple only in theory. Using Avar Kriss's ability to link minds with the Force, all of the Jedi would reach out to find the object. By applying the Force in precisely the same spot at the same time, they could move the container just enough to divert its path toward the sun. Yet for such a simple plan, the task ahead of them was enormously challenging. There were great distances between the Jedi, and the object was moving so quickly. If the Jedi were not careful, they could misjudge their efforts or work against each other. Everything had to be coordinated perfectly, and even then, success was not guaranteed.

A lifetime of training is hardly enough to prepare a Jedi for the enormous strain caused by the intense focus required that day. Even for powerful Jedi, the task proved to be too much. Pilots fell unconscious while flying their ships, and others collided mid-flight. As they fell, the burden on the others grew. Yet as some became one with the Force, Avar could hear the song of other Jedi far across the galaxy who lent their focus to the effort. The Jedi were now playing into a symphony of light with Avar Kriss as their conductor. The song rose in a great crescendo, as the module was moved from its course. Hetzal had been saved.

AVAR KRISS

Avar Kriss was one of the Jedi Order's brightest lights in the age of expansion. For many, she was the shining example of what a Jedi could and should be. Kriss exhibited a rare combination of natural talent and hard work since she was a Padawan, and thus quickly rose

ABOVE Avar Kriss, Marshal of Starlight Beacon.

through the ranks to become a Jedi Master earlier than most. Kriss forged a deep friendship with Elzar Mann and Stellan Gios in their formative years as Padawans. Though they studied under individual masters, the three regularly trained and conducted missions together. The three firebrands, as they came to be known, were individually talented, but together, they were truly exceptional in both the Force and their ability to cause trouble. Under the guidance of Master Cherff Maota, Kriss honed her ability to connect with others in these years, while also proving herself a capable duelist and leader. As the Padawan of a Jedi Seeker who frequently traveled the galaxy, Avar had long been interested in pursuing a posting where she could make a difference in the Outer Rim. However, she could not have anticipated just how critical she would be to this corner of the galaxy.

By the will of the Force, Avar Kriss was among the Jedi delayed leaving Starlight Beacon when the *Legacy Run* disaster struck. Her role conducting the Jedi rescue effort became legendary, earning her the title "the Hero of Hetzal," and affording her galaxy-wide fame that was rare among the Order. Following the Great Disaster, Master Kriss led the investigation of the Emergences that continued to plague the Outer Rim, a highly visible role among the Jedi Council and Republic chancellor's office alike.

Avar Kriss's exceptional leadership earned her the surprise posting as the marshal of Starlight Beacon, a position that was once filled by Master Jora Malli. After Malli's untimely death at Kur, Kriss was handed the role shortly before the station's dedication ceremony. But over the following months, Marshal Kriss was increasingly drawn away from her station to investigate

a growing Drengir threat and the persistent antagonism of the Nihil.

Avar Kriss was pragmatic at her core, a trait that could bring her into conflict with the more idealistic members of the Order. When she embarked to repel the Drengir scourge, she set her mind to defeating them at any cost, even if it meant forging unlikely alliances with former enemies. While those far from the battle might have criticized her approach, those who fought alongside her never questioned what must be done.

She had little time to celebrate her victory over the Drengir at Mulita, when Nihil raiders struck at Valo, leading Marshal Kriss to once again go on the offensive. As the leader of Operation Counterstrike, she collected victory after victory against the scattered Nihil forces. But like a nest of scurriers, the Nihil would slip through the cracks and reemerge no matter how many had been eliminated. The ordeal put Avar Kriss under intense and prolonged pressure, straining her relationships with the Council and the Jedi closest to her. Some around her were left to wonder if her intense sense of duty and desire to right the galaxy's wrongs would cloud her judgment or worse, undermine her greatest strengths. But for the galaxy at large, Avar Kriss will always be remembered as the great Hero of Hetzal.

THE BATTLE OF KUR

Before the Great Disaster, the Kur Nebula was just another point in the vastness of deep space. It soon became the site of the first major battle between the Republic and the Nihil.

Once the Republic discovered that the Nihil were behind the *Legacy Run* disaster, Lina Soh called for swift justice to meet the Nihil fleet head on in battle. Jedi participation in any offensive effort was a contentious issue among the High Council, with some arguing that offensive strikes were not the way of the Jedi. But the decided vote came down on the side of action, so the Jedi joined the Republic task force.

The Republic Defense Coalition, a volunteer force of ships and crews from prosperous Republic worlds, was prepared for one of the largest engagements in decades. The treaty worlds were all eager for the chance to strike back at the Nihil following the Great Hyperspace Disaster, and their confidence was further bolstered by the presence of the Jedi Order's *Ataraxia*. Sweeping and sleek for its size, the *Ataraxia* was like a temple in the skies. Many of the Jedi on board had heroically served at Hetzal and were keenly aware of how important their presence was to securing peace for the Outer Rim.

They faced a sizable Nihil force led by Tempest Runner Kassav Milliko aboard his flagship, the *New Elite*, protected by a hundred or so smaller Strikeships, Cloudships, assault crafts, and fighters cobbled together into a frightening frenzy of a fleet. The haphazard collection of vessels and technology was nonetheless well-armed for the conflict to come.

Although the Nihil forces were routed that day, the Republic victory came at a great cost.

The Republic and the Jedi learned for the first time who they were dealing with: a brutal, chaotic enemy whose tactics spared no one. The Nihil released radioactive poison, killing Republic pilots and Nihil alike. And just as defeat seemed imminent, the Nihil began using their Path engines to engage in seemingly impossible micro-jumps.

Blinking in and out of hyperspace, the Nihil were a challenge even for the Jedi to counter. These soon devolved into suicide attacks, as Nihil ships went crashing into the Republic fleet. The Jedi there that day sensed nothing but fear and terror among them, as if the Nihil were helpless as their ships came crashing into their enemies.

JORA MALLI

The brutality of the Battle of Kur took the Jedi by surprise, taking with it one of the galaxy's finest Jedi Masters. Jora Malli was to be the first commander of the Jedi Quarter on Starlight Beacon, but the Togruta never got her chance to serve as the station's first marshal. Malli believed in action, often choosing to be away from the Grand Temple, even during her appointment to the High Council. She was more comfortable out in the galaxy, doing good, rather than sitting in a tower. It was a posting that would play to her diplomatic strengths, as the station would be a hub of activity for systems throughout the frontier. She felt that leaving Coruscant would be good for her Padawan, Reath Silas, as well, but Malli was tragically killed at Kur. She became one with the Force while piloting her Vector in battle, taking action as she always had, rather than watching from the safety of the *Ataraxia*.

TAKING FLIGHT: THE JEDI AND THEIR VECTORS

While a Jedi has many remarkable abilities, flight is rarely one of them. In those cases where a Jedi must take to the skies, they often rely on a nimble craft known as the Vector. This single- or two-seater craft is built to be interchangeable between

ABOVE Jora Malli at the Battle of Kur.

their Jedi operators, with the accommodating cockpits allowing smaller Jedi like Yoda or towering Wookiees like Arkoff to take the controls with minimal modification. Vectors do not have an integrated hyperdrive, but they can travel at light speed with the addition of a triangular hyperframe whose built-in navidroid assists with jump calculations.

The Vector's classification would fall under what other forces might consider a starfighter, but the Vector is not designed purely with combat in mind. Their dual cannons operate without a targeting computer and can be adjusted to nonlethal power if desired. To fly a Vector in combat, the pilot needs just one thing: their

lightsaber. Unlike the Republic's Skyhawk interceptors, the Vector uses a lightsaber as the key to its weapon systems. Placing a lightsaber in the activation panel requires a Jedi to carefully consider what comes next. Violence should be the last resort of a Jedi, and only used in the defense of others. With this added security measure, the Jedi pilot must be sure that laser cannons are the only option.

The beauty of the Vector lies not in heavy shielding, powerful weapons, or advanced technology. It has very little of all of those things. Instead, the Vector is small and nimble, virtually an extension of its Jedi pilot. The ship is so sparsely armored and automated that only a Force-user has the reflexes to effectively pilot it. Their strength is not in their abundant technology but rather in their ability to work as a multiplier of the Jedi's own abilities.

And when they fly together, Jedi pilots are truly unmatched. A fleet flying together was known as a Drift of Vectors, a feat of coordination that goes far beyond formation flying. A Drift could bridge minds through the Force, allowing them to coordinate every movement far beyond what ordinary pilots could achieve. Through this Force connection, a Drift moves as one.

The Vector has become a common sight in the Outer Rim as the Jedi defend the frontier from the Nihil. They helped clear debris and rescue survivors at Hetzal. Vectors served to defend key Republic shipyards at Cyclor, and protect the citizens of Port Haileap, but it is not a starship alone that wins battles. It is the pairing of ship, Jedi, and the Force that makes these things possible.

THE DEDICATION OF STARLIGHT BEACON

With the Great Hyperspace Disaster, the Emergences, and the Battle of Kur behind them, never was there a more appropriate time to recommit the Republic and the Jedi to their shared mission of peace, hope, and prosperity. The dedication of Starlight Beacon provided just that, with a ceremony to mark the opening of Chancellor Lina Soh's greatest of the Great Works.

Standing there in the central assembly room at the heart of Starlight Beacon, it was impossible to not get caught up in the emotion of that day. Everything the Republic stood for was on display. Countless species stood united, representing planets from the deep Core to the furthest reaches of the frontier. Scientists, engineers, doctors, and teachers stood alongside senators, ministers, and royalty. Every prominent member of the Jedi Order was there that day, dressed in their finest white ceremonial robes. They were there not just as partners to the Republic but to present a salute of vibrant color, igniting their lightsabers at the very moment Starlight Beacon was activated.

It had been said thousands of times before that moment, but at that very second, it rang truer than ever: We are all the Republic.

STARLIGHT AND THE DALNA CATACLYSM

After its dedication, Starlight Beacon instantly became a vibrant hub of activity for the Republic in the Outer Rim. From this towering space station, the Republic offered refuge and resources for all who came. Its medcenter, staffed with some of the finest doctors, surgeons, and medical technology the Republic could offer, took in the mounting sick or wounded. And with new foes seemingly around every turn as the Republic expanded further into the Outer Rim, every bed was needed.

The station also served as a hub for ensuring peace in this untamed part of the galaxy. Starlight was well equipped for the Republic to stage countless missions to prevent piracy, deter smuggling, and of course, combat the Nihil and Drengir threat. The Jedi of Starlight Beacon rarely had time to rest between the staggering number of missions they conducted. Marshal Kriss personally led the defense against the Drengir and Operation Counterstrike against the Nihil, racking up hard-earned victories in numerous systems.

When a catastrophe struck the planet Dalna, simply sending rescuers was no longer an option.

Dalna fell victim to a terrifying new Nihil weapon powered by synthetic kyber crystals. Groundquakes unleashed a chain reaction of volcanic eruptions powerful enough to raise the planet's temperature by several degrees. Dormant volcanoes rumbled to life once again, signaling that in a matter of weeks, the entire planet would be covered in lava. With the cataclysm threatening all of Dalna's citizens and not enough ships to evacuate them in time, a bold idea came from an unlikely source: the young Padawan Imri Cantaros. Imri suggested that Starlight Beacon—the *entire* Starlight Beacon—might be the solution.

If the station could travel to Dalna, there would be plenty of room and resources to save the small planet's population. Since Starlight's hyperspace engines were not yet fully operational, Knight Lyssa Votz offered up an approach used in days past when not all ships had hyperdrives. It was determined that other vessels should tow the massive space station to Dalna through a tandem hyperspace jump, but it would require significant power to make the maneuver. Leading this effort was the grand luxury liner *Halcyon*, fresh from its construction in the hallowed shipyards of Corellia, and amid one of its new frontier tours. Its guests had booked an exciting tour of the Outer Rim but were witness to a great feat of ingenuity and cooperation.

Starlight Beacon was a sight to behold, but together with the *Halcyon*, they were a gleaming example of Republic achievement. The arrival of these ships to save the beings of Dalna made it clear that even in the face of a cataclysm, we were living in a true golden age of the Force, the Jedi, and the Republic.

More than a century ago, Dalna was the site of a terrible tragedy involving the Jedi. Still remembered as the Night of Sorrow among local Dalnans, most Jedi have no sense of what happened, and I hesitate to even write it down.

OPPOSITE Jedi Vector cockpit interior.
INSERT Personal letter recovered on Dalna.

The *Halcyon* leads the effort to tow Starlight Beacon through hyperspace

CHAPTER 4
REPUBLIC EXPANSION

Well, Ember is very real, as is her flame.
I'd advise you to keep your distance.

— BELL ZETTIFAR

LINA SOH AND HER GREAT WORKS

The office of the supreme chancellor has ebbed and flowed over the centuries. All chancellors serve their term as the head of the Galactic Senate, but their personalities and priorities always make a unique mark upon the political office. At times, there have even been multiple chancellors, but today, the Republic is helmed by a single great leader who aims to take the government to new heights with her message of hope and unity.

Chancellor Lina Soh of Daghee was elected to her office with the promise of expanding the influence of the Republic further than it had ever been. Decades of exploration had now made it possible for new member worlds to not only be signatories to the Republic but also be truly connected to the greater galaxy. Her slogan for this was as simple as it is powerful: We are all the Republic.

Chancellor Soh had an impressive presence wherever she went. Noted for her sense of style, she managed to be both welcoming and powerful. That sense of power was assisted in no small part by her ever-present targon companions, Matari and Voru. These four-eyed, giant cats almost never left her side and were better than any security complement at deterring would-be attackers. Soh balanced being the most powerful politician in the Republic with her faithful dedication to her son, Kitrep, who was a frequent companion on her diplomatic trips across the galaxy. She had an unwavering conviction about her ideas and believed so strongly in them that she welcomed transparency more than the chancellors that came before, going so far as to allow holonet reporters to follow her during key moments.

Her spirit of unity extended to her relationship with the Jedi Order as

OPPOSITE Chancellor Lina Soh (center) with her formidable targons, Matari (left) and Voru (right).

well. The Jedi had always served at the will of the chancellor, but Lina Soh made the Jedi a partner in almost everything she did. Her Great Works, such as Starlight Beacon and the Republic Fair, all featured a significant Jedi presence. The Council believed in this partnership, but both Soh and the Jedi underestimated how some factions would reject the Republic's expansion.

A THREAT TO PEACE: THE NIHIL

Though the Republic and the Jedi were unprepared for the Nihil, citizens of the Outer Rim were no strangers to the masked band of marauders. The Outer Rim had experienced more frequent raids in the years preceding the construction of Starlight Beacon, but they had rarely attracted Jedi attention. These early attacks were more akin to sporadic acts of piracy, than the organized chaos sewn in the wake of the Great Disaster. Yet over time, the Jedi learned more about the enemy they faced and their evil ambitions for the frontier.

Now, the Nihil are far from a ragtag group of raiders, and the Jedi were surprised to learn that they maintain an organized leadership structure designed to share in the spoils of their misdeeds, and encourage growth in their ranks. At the lowest levels of the Nihil organization are Strikes, members who follow the orders of those above them. Strikes who recruit their own band of Nihil to serve under them are elevated to the level of a Cloud. Those Clouds who rose in reputation and swelled their ranks were elevated to Storm. Above them were the Tempests, led by the most vicious and ambitious among the Nihil. When one fell, there was always another to take their place. There were just three Tempest Runners and all wielded

great power among the Nihil. But though we Jedi were slow to realize it, the Tempest Runners were not the true leaders of the Nihil.

Alone at the top of the Nihil ranks was a single visionary known as the Eye of the Nihil. For a time, we believed this to be a Twi'lek named Lourna Dee, who in fact was a Tempest Runner. The Jedi hunted her, but she eluded our grasp time and again. Yet while we were distracted by chasing Dee, the true leader of the Nihil hid in the shadows. He is Marchion Ro, a figure that we still know little about. What is clear is that he holds a deep hatred for the Jedi, and rebukes the Republic's expansion into the Outer Rim. The Great Disaster, the tragedy at Valo, and the fate of Starlight Beacon were all his doing. He gathered a tight grip upon the Nihil by controlling the knowledge of secret hyperspace lanes, known to Ro as the "Paths." It was these seemingly impossible hyperspace jumps that made the Nihil so effective at evading us, and allowed Ro to control such an unruly band of raiders.

The allure of the Nihil is almost incomprehensible to the Jedi, as it is so contrary to what the Order upholds. The Nihil embrace anarchy and chaos. They welcome the downtrodden, murderous, and greedy by offering freedom above all else. Freedom to "ride the storm" to wealth and pleasure. Freedom to hide behind a chilling mask and take whatever they want from others. Despite the horrors they have inflicted on the galaxy, and despite the success the Jedi have had in apprehending them, still more take to the Paths to rain despair and destruction in the name of the Eye.

The horrors of a Nihil raid.

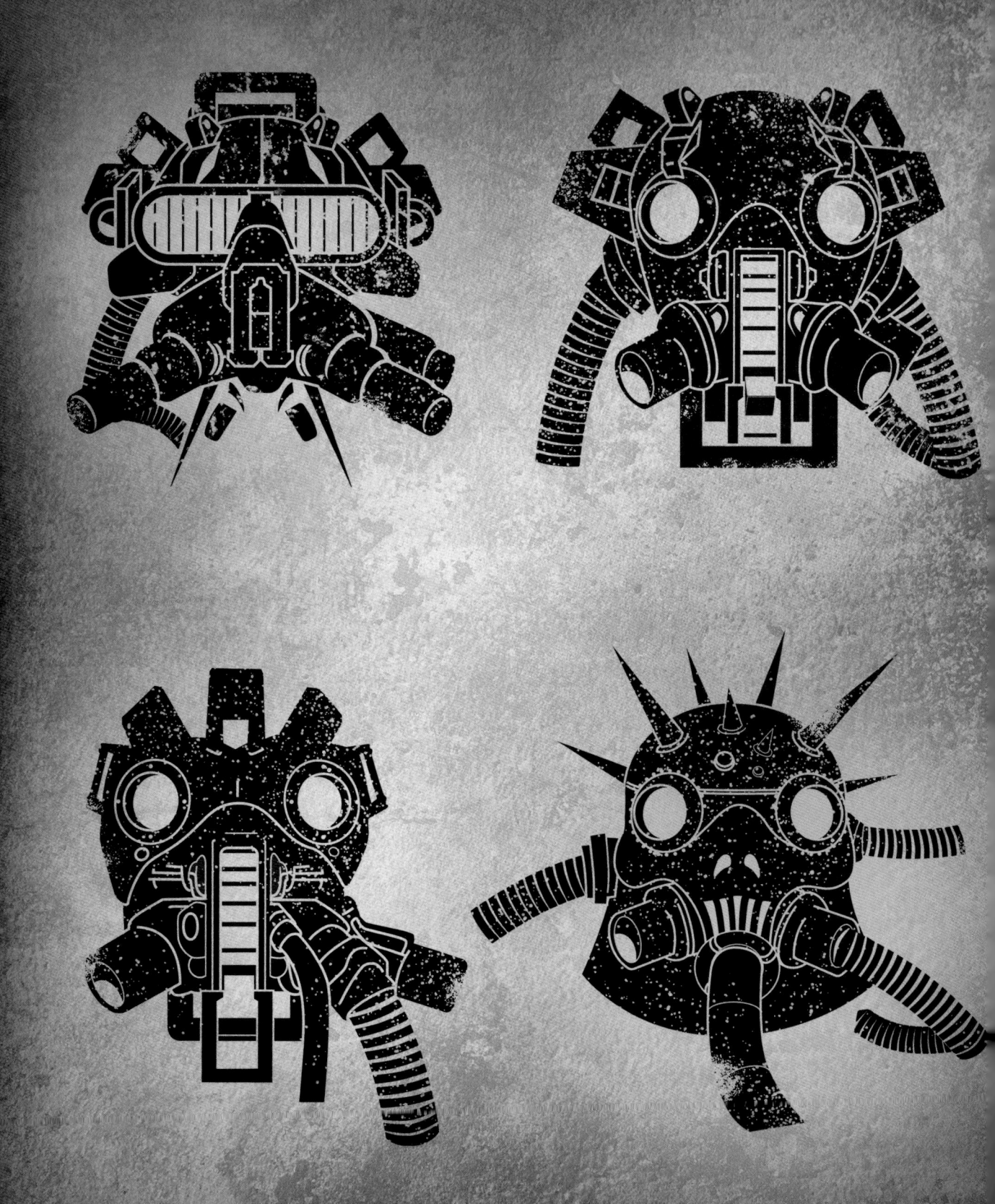

NIHIL TACTICS AND TECHNOLOGY

With every encounter with the Nihil, the Jedi learned valuable insights about how they fought. For a band of nomadic pirates, these raiders were surprisingly well-equipped. Where technology could not account for their shortcomings, their savagery was left to suffice.

The trademark tactic of the Nihil was their warcloud, a noxious gas leveled on the battlefield to incapacitate their enemies. The Nihil wore masks not only to conceal their identities and scare their enemies but also to protect the raiders from the gas's harmful effects.

Their poisonous gas was just one of the dastardly tactics the Nihil employed. Their razor-sharp harpoons were used to capture unarmed ships. Captains who did not submit had their vessels pulled apart by the harpoon tow cables, and their crews exposed to the vacuum of space. Nihil captains would dump radioactive material in their wake to poison fellow pilots, or lay ambushes with fake distress calls. Their arsenal is ever evolving, and scav droids are a seemingly new addition to the Nihil arsenal, but they proved devastating at Rekelos and Valo. The scav droids' mandible arms can cut and tear apart a ship's hull into shreds, exposing valuable loot or terrified crew. The invention of mole mines, tiny bombs that spring up from the ground when detonated, caused unspeakable injuries to ground forces who stumbled upon these indiscriminate explosives.

The Nihil would have never grown to be more than a band of local raiders had it not been for their fleet of ships. Each Tempest Runner kept their own flagship. These were supported by a number of large Stormships and Cloudships, themselves protected by fighter-like Strikeships. Aside from their brutal appearance and sometimes similar markings, each ship in the Nihil fleet is different. Many looked like they had been cobbled together from pieces of other vessels, and some were outfitted to merge with other Nihil ships to form larger crafts. All were designed to strike fear into their

OPPOSITE Nihil masks.

THIS PAGE (left to right) Nihil Tempest Runners Kara Xoo and Zeetar.

targets, but it was not their size or their arsenals that made them so effective.

Nihil ships are constructed around a special Path engine. Similar to how other ships might have a hyperdrive to propel the ship into hyperspace, Path engines make jumps those other ships would find impossible. The Nihil use this ability to strike targets without warning, then jump away again, seemingly at will. While standard vessels make complicated and time-consuming calculations, a Nihil Path ship would be gone in an instant.

The exact function of Path engines remains a mystery, but it is believed they are powered by time-phased calculations. Others suggest that they make their jumps using unmapped routes unknown to the wider galaxy. The Paths allow the Nihil to jump into hyperspace through places that seem impossible, places where the gravity would interfere with even the most advanced navigation computer or droid.

Captured Nihil vessels offer little clues as to how the Paths truly function. Our best engineers haven't found an explanation within the hardware itself for these phenomenal jumps. We can only speculate that the source of the Paths lies elsewhere, and that is what gives the Eye of the Nihil such power over the seething raiders.

THESE PAGES Marchion Ro (left) and Nihil Tempest Runners Pan Eyta, Kassav Milliko, and Lourna Dee.

LODEN GREATSTORM AND BELL ZETTIFAR

Loden Greatstorm was among the finest teachers in the Jedi Order, even if his methods could be at times unsettling for his students. The Twi'lek master had taken multiple Padawans throughout his lifetime and approached each of them in the same way. He saw every moment as a learning opportunity. "If I do everything, no one learns anything," he would famously say, often before putting his Padawan through the next challenge in an endless gauntlet of nearly impossible tasks. The life of a Greatstorm apprentice meant being pushed off of tall buildings or having to calm a charging monster while the master stood back and observed.

Greatstorm had a knack for choosing fine Padawans who could survive and thrive through

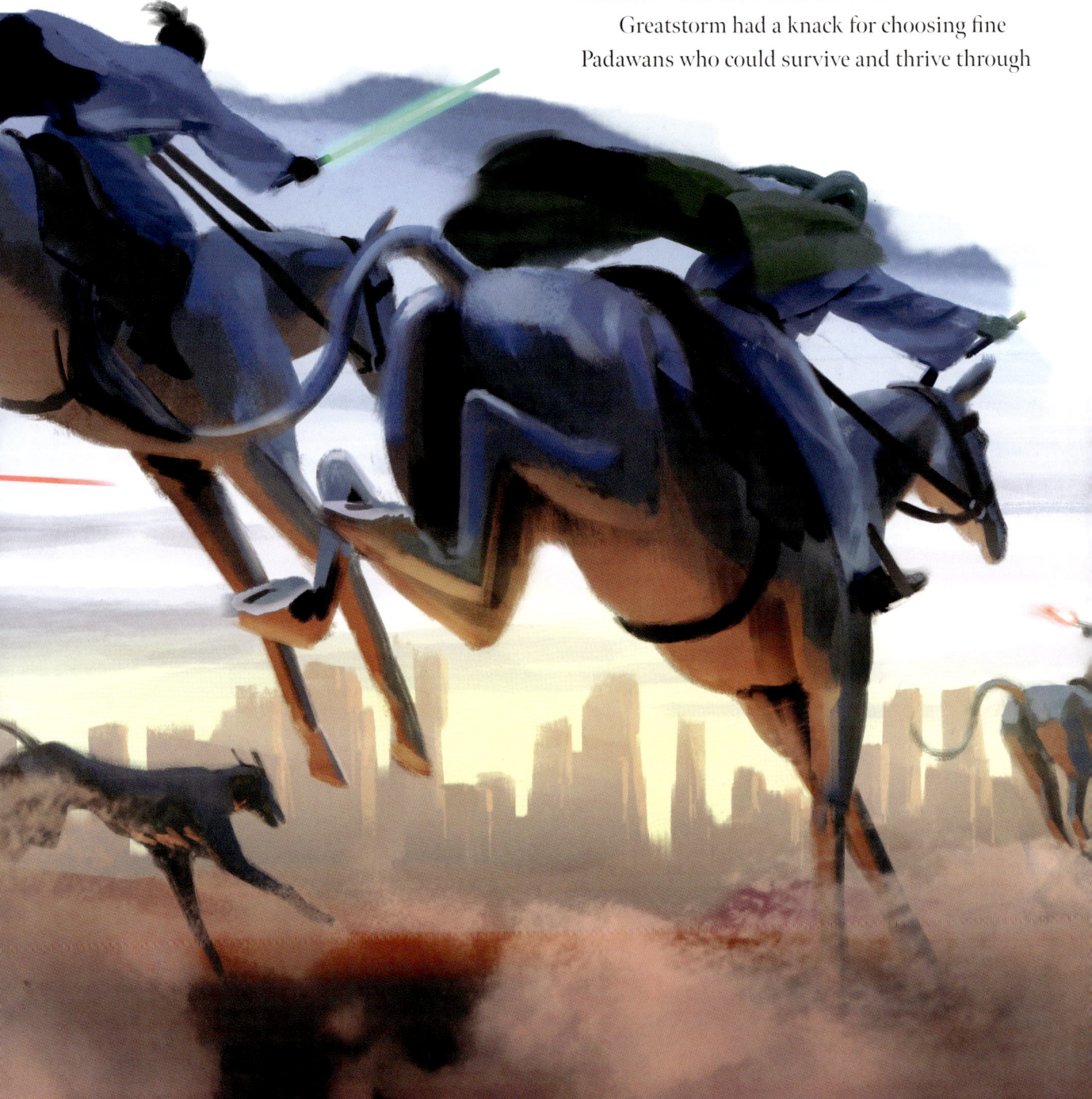

his teachings. Time and again, they emerged as Knights more prepared than any other. Years of hands-on training forged them into fine leaders and masters in their own right, spreading a legacy of Greatstorm's lessons far across the Order.

Loden Greatstorm's most recent Padawan was Bell Zettifar, a human whose indomitable spirit was put to the test every day by his master's challenging trials. Similar training might have broken less capable Padawans, but Zettifar rose to the challenge time and again. While Greatstorm was a caring master, his Padawan found more comfort from his other constant companion, a charhound he named Ember. The elegant creature was a native of Elphrona and taken in by the Jedi of that temple. After attending to the wounded animal, the creature simply never left when the Jedi all became quite fond of her. Ember is loving and loyal, rarely displaying her species' naturally high internal body temperature, which allows

them to exhale flames. Considering that Bell Zettifar sees the Force as a flame, it is perhaps no coincidence that his destiny is shared with a creature that runs so hot.

The duo of Greatstorm and Zettifar served heroically at Hetzal. As debris from the *Legacy Run* threatened the planet, the Jedi raced to the surface in their Vector where Zettifar's intuition guided them to the compound of a wealthy family. Local farmers had gathered outside the compound gates in the hopes of boarding the family's ship to escape, but the farmers found themselves endangered by selfishness in more ways than one. The Jedi duo first defended the farmers from raiders who pounced on the defenseless citizens, and then they persuaded the wealthy shipowners to allow the less privileged to board.

Back at home on their outpost world of Elphrona, master and apprentice encountered the Nihil face-to-face for the first time. Greatstorm and Zettifar answered a distress call to assist a local family in danger of being kidnapped. The duo, along with Porter Engle and Indeera Stokes, raced to the rescue only to discover that it was a Nihil trap. Loden Greatstorm was believed to be killed in the action, though Bell suspected he might have survived. The ordeal left Bell's confidence shaken despite his admirable performance in rescuing the kidnapped family. If the Nihil could defeat a truly great Jedi Master like Loden Greatstorm, what was in store for everyone else?

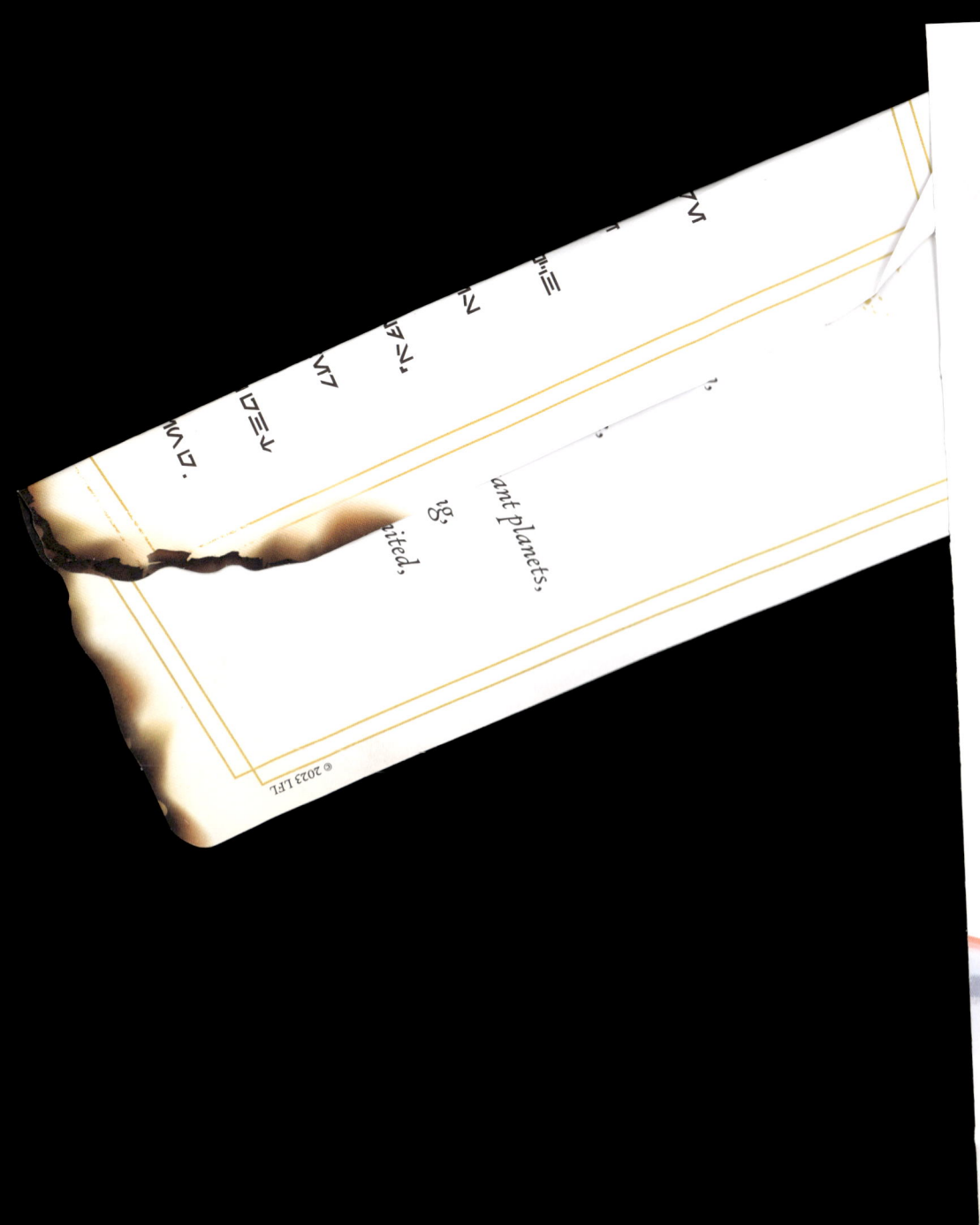

LEFT Jedi Zettifar and Greatstorm attempt to rescue a family on Elphrona from Nihil kidnappers.

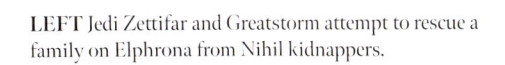

THE REPUBLIC FAIR

The Republic Fair on Valo was to be the physical manifestation of Chancellor Lina Soh's "Spirit of Unity." The planet Valo played host to the first such fair in generations, which Chancellor Soh felt strongly would inspire the entire Republic by showcasing the very best that cooperation had produced. The chancellor was involved in every detail and viewed the event as her next Great Work.

The fair had many components. Valo's capital, Lonisa City, was essentially taken over by the fair. The city's hotels became housing for visitors and dignitaries, and the imported tree-lined main street, Republic Avenue, was the chief thoroughfare, guiding visitors to the many exhibits and pavilions.

To display the wide array of Republic achievements, the fair had four distinct exhibition zones each centered around a theme: Technology and Science, Sport and Adventure, Arts and Culture, and finally, Faith and Life.

The Faith and Life pavilion was a celebration of the Force. As the real Starlight operated in space far from Valo, this pavilion conveyed the Republic's vision and ambition for the station. The Jedi Order contributed its own exhibit titled Secrets of the Jedi, complete with artifacts shipped in from Coruscant, Devaron, and Starlight Beacon itself. The Faith and Life zone was also home to the United in Song exhibit, whose chorus had already earned a reputation for being dangerously catchy.

The antigrav fountains were a stunning highlight of the Arts and Culture zone. In the Technology and Science zone, displays ranged from peaceful botanical gardens to a display of cutting-edge defense equipment. The Sport and Adventure zone welcomed visitors to watch or participate in a variety of games made popular in Republic star systems, though Jedi were not allowed to participate on account of their exceptional abilit[...]

From Republic Avenue, visitors could catc[...] a transport to any one of the forty-two floatin[...] World Pavilions installed for the fair. These manufactured platforms revolved the large[...] platform of them all, that which represent[...] Coruscant. But even those who didn't ca[...] big-city theme of the Coruscant pavilion would find something among the other Republic member planets who hosted platforms. Onderon offered jungle safaris, Spira hosted beach escapes, and Hetzal served fruits—a reminder of the Jedi's actions during the Great Disaster.

Visitors flocked to the pavilions and platforms to see the magnificent exhibits. There, the wealth and grandeur of the Core Worlds was on display alongside the hopeful idealism of the Outer Rim. The Lonisa City Zoo offered a quieter escape amid its walking paths and wildlife displays. To make the zoo even more impressive, fair organizers imported animals from across the Republic, including a number of apex predators.

ABOVE The Unity Arc.

INSERT Chorus lyrics from the United in Song exhibit, recovered from the Republic Fair wreckage.

OPPOSITE Fairgoers marvel at purebred fathiers imported from a Republic member world.

THE REPUBLIC FAIR

The Republic Fair on Valo was to be the physical manifestation of Chancellor Lina Soh's "Spirit of Unity." The planet Valo played host to the first such fair in generations, which Chancellor Soh felt strongly would inspire the entire Republic by showcasing the very best that cooperation had produced. The chancellor was involved in every detail and viewed the event as her next Great Work.

The fair had many components. Valo's capital, Lonisa City, was essentially taken over by the fair. The city's hotels became housing for visitors and dignitaries, and the imported tree-lined main street, Republic Avenue, was the chief thoroughfare, guiding visitors to the many exhibits and pavilions.

To display the wide array of Republic achievements, the fair had four distinct exhibition zones each centered around a theme: Technology and Science, Sport and Adventure, Arts and Culture, and finally, Faith and Life.

The Faith and Life pavilion was a celebration of the Force. As the real Starlight operated in space far from Valo, this pavilion conveyed the Republic's vision and ambition for the station. The Jedi Order contributed its own exhibit titled Secrets of the Jedi, complete with artifacts shipped in from Coruscant, Devaron, and Starlight Beacon itself. The Faith and Life zone was also home to the United in Song exhibit, whose chorus had already earned a reputation for being dangerously catchy.

The antigrav fountains were a stunning highlight of the Arts and Culture zone. In the Technology and Science zone, displays ranged from peaceful botanical gardens to a display of cutting-edge defense equipment. The Sport and Adventure zone welcomed visitors to watch or participate in a variety of games made popular in Republic star systems, though Jedi were not allowed to participate on account of their exceptional abilities.

From Republic Avenue, visitors could catch a transport to any one of the forty-two floating World Pavilions installed for the fair. These manufactured platforms revolved the largest platform of them all, that which represented Coruscant. But even those who didn't care for the big-city theme of the Coruscant pavilion would find something among the other Republic member planets who hosted platforms. Onderon offered jungle safaris, Spira hosted beach escapes, and Hetzal served fruits—a reminder of the Jedi's actions during the Great Disaster.

Visitors flocked to the pavilions and platforms to see the magnificent exhibits. There, the wealth and grandeur of the Core Worlds was on display alongside the hopeful idealism of the Outer Rim. The Lonisa City Zoo offered a quieter escape amid its walking paths and wildlife displays. To make the zoo even more impressive, fair organizers imported animals from across the Republic, including a number of apex predators.

ABOVE The Unity Arc.

INSERT Chorus lyrics from the United in Song exhibit, recovered from the Republic Fair wreckage.

OPPOSITE Fairgoers marvel at purebred fathiers imported from a Republic member world.

his teachings. Time and again, they emerged as Knights more prepared than any other. Years of hands-on training forged them into fine leaders and masters in their own right, spreading a legacy of Greatstorm's lessons far across the Order.

Loden Greatstorm's most recent Padawan was Bell Zettifar, a human whose indominable spirit was put to the test every day by his master's challenging trials. Similar training might have broken less capable Padawans, but Zettifar rose to the challenge time and again. While Greatstorm was a caring master, his Padawan found more comfort from his other constant companion, a charhound he named Ember. The elegant creature was a native of Elphrona and taken in by the Jedi of that temple. After attending to the wounded animal, the creature simply never left when the Jedi all became quite fond of her. Ember is loving and loyal, rarely displaying her species' naturally high internal body temperature, which allows

them to exhale flames. Considering that Bell Zettifar sees the Force as a flame, it is perhaps no coincidence that his destiny is shared with a creature that runs so hot.

The duo of Greatstorm and Zettifar served heroically at Hetzal. As debris from the *Legacy Run* threatened the planet, the Jedi raced to the surface in their Vector where Zettifar's intuition guided them to the compound of a wealthy family. Local farmers had gathered outside the compound gates in the hopes of boarding the family's ship to escape, but the farmers found themselves endangered by selfishness in more ways than one. The Jedi duo first defended the farmers from raiders who pounced on the defenseless citizens, and then they persuaded the wealthy shipowners to allow the less privileged to board.

Back at home on their outpost world of Elphrona, master and apprentice encountered the Nihil face-to-face for the first time. Greatstorm and Zettifar answered a distress call to assist a local family in danger of being kidnapped. The duo, along with Porter Engle and Indeera Stokes, raced to the rescue only to discover that it was a Nihil trap. Loden Greatstorm was believed to be killed in the action, though Bell suspected he might have survived. The ordeal left Bell's confidence shaken despite his admirable performance in rescuing the kidnapped family. If the Nihil could defeat a truly great Jedi Master like Loden Greatstorm, what was in store for everyone else?

LEFT Jedi Zettifar and Greatstorm attempt to rescue a family on Elphrona from Nihil kidnappers.

The Unity Arc offered history buffs and art lovers an impressive display to honor the Core Founders of the Republic. An arching collection of twenty-two spheres towered far above the grand avenue, each sphere representing one of the founding members of the Republic. The arc was precisely placed to encourage visitors to gaze up to the skies in astonishment, looking out to the impressive World Pavilions. But their awe was soon replaced by terror, for before their eyes, chaos rained down upon the Republic Fair.

THE NIHIL STRIKE

The Valo fair was supposed to be a turning point in the course of Republic history. It was a spectacle so grand and inspiring that it would be remembered in the coming centuries as the defining moment that unified the galaxy unlike never before. The opening ceremony was a fitting celebration that welcomed visitors from across the galaxy. Speeches were made, starfighters streaked in formation overhead, and the wondrous research vessel the *Innovator* arrived to thunderous applause. As the crowds sprawled into the various pavilions, they could truly feel a renewed spirit of unity. But it wasn't long before the Jedi felt a more ominous sensation through the Force.

As civilian ships lined up in the atmosphere to arrive at the fair for its second day, a great explosion tore through the sky. Arriving out of nowhere, the Nihil had used the Paths to jump into Valo's atmosphere without warning. Their Strikes,

THESE PAGES Stellan Gios wields two lightsabers—his signature blue-bladed saber, and the green-bladed saber of his former Master, Rana Kant. Dignitaries from across the galaxy shelter within the Rothana experimental walker, as Master Gios deflects the Nihil attack.

Clouds, and Storms spread out across the fair with some targeting the floating World Pavilions, others strafing ground targets, and yet another group holding back to ambush any ship attempting to leave the system. The chaos was made worse by a communications blackout that left the defenders unable to get signals off planet for help, nor communicate with Jedi across the planet.

The destruction of the fair was rapid and thorough. The Nihil were not well organized, but their superior numbers and careless attacks caused terrible losses. Half of the fair's magnificent World Pavilion platforms came crashing down after the first wave of the assault. Soon, Nihil marauders led by Lourna Dee took to the ground to loot and kill with their noxious warcloud providing cover as they moved through Lonisa City. We now know they had one goal in mind: killing Chancellor Lina Soh.

The Jedi in attendance did what they could to mount a defense, but they were shorthanded for such a fight. The ongoing struggle against the Drengir called all available Jedi to Mulita, leaving only a token number of the Order to attend the opening of the fair. Some took to the skies in their Vectors, while Stellan Gios worked to protect Lina Soh and her visiting dignitaries. Elzar Mann moved through a city made dangerous by the escape of dangerous predators from the zoo exhibits. All fought bravely, but there were simply not enough Jedi to repel the attack. If the Jedi were going to save those that still survived, they had to find a way to call Starlight Beacon for help.

OPPOSITE Ram Jomaram with V-18 and some Bonbraks.

RAM JOMARAM

Ram Jomaram was an unlikely hero of the Republic Fair. This young Padawan was born on Valo where he studied under Master Kunpar Vasivola, whose patient ways were a fit for this nontraditional learner. Ram Jomaram is a tinkerer at heart. His robes are almost always covered in engine grease or droid fluids, a sign that he feels most comfortable in a garage rather than a temple chamber. His time as a Padawan on the frontier saw him forge unique friendships with his droid, V-18, and pack of sentient creatures native to Valo known as Bonbraks. It was his penchant for technology and his native knowledge of the planet's infrastructure that led him into the center of the events of the fair.

The morning of the opening ceremonies, as elder Jedi stood by during Lina Soh's dedication, Padawan Ram noticed something was amiss at Crashpoint Tower, a communications station that serviced Lonisa City and beyond. Ram raced to warn the Jedi of the disturbance, but he was mistaken for an intruder and captured by an overbearing law enforcer. As he sat in his detention cell, the attack Ram hoped to warn them about got underway. Yet, his spirit was not broken by this disappointment. Young Ram enlisted the assistance of his fellow Padawans and returned to Crashpoint Tower, discovering the cause of the planet's communication disruption.

To everyone's astonishment, the Nihil had planted Drengir spores at the tower. These two terrible enemies were now working together, and it was the Drengir infestation that had interrupted planetary comms. Ram was not an exceptional duelist, nor could he and the Padawans have overpowered the carnivorous plants. Instead, the

crafty Padawan convinced the Drengir that they were being betrayed by their Nihil allies, turning them against each other. Ram personally restored the planetary communications, just in time for the Jedi to regroup and repel the Nihil warcloud.

Ram's natural talents with technology continue to serve the Force. Whether reprogramming scav droids on Valo or his bravery to save others on Corellia, this young Jedi is proof that talents take many forms. Ram Jomaram simply brings light to the galaxy in his own unique way.

BELL ZETTIFAR AT THE *INNOVATOR*

The *Innovator* was the latest of Lina Soh's Great Works. One of the most sophisticated crafts in the Republic, the *Elite*-class vessel was a pioneer ship set to explore and map previously uncharted areas of space. The *Innovator* was to be the first in a new fleet of science vessels designed to expand the Republic's knowledge of the galaxy in ways not seen since the Great Hyperspace Rush.

Initially, the Nihil attempted to destroy the ship while it was completing final preparations at the Cyclor shipyards. Though Bell Zettifar was wounded in his starfighter attempting to defend the important vessel, the Jedi and Cyclorrians successfully repelled the attack. The *Innovator* was prepped for its grand debut at the Republic Fair.

The arrival of the *Innovator* was the crowning moment in the fair's opening ceremonies. It docked over Lake Lonisa on the shores of Lonisa City, prepared to welcome lines of visitors eager to say they were among the first to see the shining new ship. Its arrival was a stark reminder for Bell Zettifar of the suffering that he had experienced in the past: first, the loss of his master, Loden

Greatstorm, followed by his grievous injuries at the Cyclor shipyards defending the *Innovator* from a Nihil attack. Bell had spent considerable time in a bacta tank recovering from his injuries at Cyclor. The new therapy healed his body, but the experience left far too much time to obsess over past traumas.

On the second day of the fair, Zettifar returned to the *Innovator* in search of Kitrep Soh, son of the chancellor, who had snuck off to the great ship with a friend. Shortly after Bell arrived with his charhound companion, so did the Nihil. When they appeared overhead, the *Innovator*'s decks were crowded with tourists, every one of them exposed to the attack that soon arrived. As he called for an evacuation of the external platforms, the Nihil fighters reached the *Innovator*. An explosion sent Bell tumbling into a gaping hole created in the ship's hull. The *Innovator* was damaged and taking on water from the lake below, with Bell and many others now entombed inside.

When Bell found Kitrep and others, they were trapped inside the *Innovator*'s shuttle bay. Their attempt to blast their way out aboard a shuttle was hampered by a large beam in their path. Bell arrived just in time to rescue the survivors, using his lightsaber to cut through the barrier and allowing the shuttle to escape as Bell clung to the outside. They emerged from the sinking *Innovator*, saved by the bravery of a Jedi. Bell lost his lightsaber in the effort, but the physical loss was nothing compared to the emotional strain that was mounting inside of him. Bell's journey would grow more challenging still.

OPPOSITE Bell Zettifar rescues survivors by holding up the wreckage of the *Innovator*.

Though the *Innovator* and many souls aboard were lost, the magnificent ship offered one final triumph for the Republic. Vam Targes, the famed designer of the *Innovator*, made a scientific breakthrough using the vessel's cutting-edge technology—the brilliant scientist developed a method to predict Nihil incursions. Unfortunately, Targes was among those who perished when the *Innovator* sunk, but Bell's knowledge of this newfound technology led Republic recovery teams to rescue the Targes' findings from the sunken wreckage. Thanks to Bell Zettifar, the promise of the *Innovator* lives on.

ABOVE Indeera Stokes pilots a Vector.
OPPOSITE PAGE Jedi Vectors fly the Sunburris cascade maneuver.

INDEERA STOKES

Jedi Knight Indeera Stokes, a kind and selfless Jedi who served at the Elphrona temple outpost, became renowned after the events of the Great Disaster as one of the finest pilots in the Jedi Order. Indeera was a natural behind the controls of a machine, whether driving a Vanguard across rocky terrain or taking to the skies in her Vector starship. She made piloting look easy even in some of the most challenging circumstances.

A fine example of this grace was on exhibit during the Nihil raid on Elphrona. As a team of Jedi led by Loden Greatstorm raced to free a kidnapped family from the marauders, Indeera Stokes used the Force to fly two Vectors at once, successfully warding off a Nihil air attack that threatened her fellow Jedi. A Vector is designed to be controlled through the Force if needed, but flying two at the same time was a spectacular feat of concentration.

Loden Greatstorm did not return from that battle, leaving his Padawan Bell Zettifar without a master. Indeera Stokes had hoped to spend her time studying the Force-reactive properties of essurtanium found on the planet, but the Nihil scourge and Greatstorm's untimely death led her to volunteer as Zettifar's new master.

The year that followed was a challenging one for them both, though Stokes proved herself a capable mentor for Bell through increasingly difficult times. When the Nihil attacked the Cyclor shipyards prior to the Republic Fair, Indeera was key to their defense. When a Nihil harpoon shattered Zettifar's cockpit, Stokes saved her Padawan's life by miraculously using the Force to patch the hole, while still flying her own Vector in the heat of battle. Soon thereafter, Indeera flew at the Republic Fair, leading the air defense against

the deadly attack, and later leading the infiltration of the Nihil complex on Grizal alongside her Padawan—a mission that is counted among one of the Republic's greatest victories over the marauders.

FLIGHT FOR THE LIGHT

NIB ASSEK

The jovial and kind personality of Nib Assek does not betray the seasoned warrior she really was. Assek was a fine duelist, but her ability shone most brightly behind the controls of a Vector. She was among the Order's finest formation flyers and was thus invited to lead the flyover of Lonisa City during the Republic Fair's opening ceremonies.

Her most recent Padawan was the Wookiee Burryaga, a rare species in the Order. To facilitate her apprentice, she learned his native tongue of Shyriiwook, a sign of her deep commitment to her task.

Sanvals carry Elzar Mann and Ty Yorrick into battle above Valo.

MIKKEL SUTMANI

The Ithorian Jedi Knight Mikkel Sutmani was a veteran of the Jedi actions at Hetzal and the following missions to uncover the cause of the Great Disaster. A fine pilot in his own right, Sutmani became one with the Force while exhibiting the best of what a Jedi should be. During the Battle of Valo when the Nihil attacked the Republic Fair, Sutmani was among the Jedi who mounted the air defense over Lonisa City. As the Drift flew to rescue survivors falling from the flying World Pavilions, Mikkel rescued a Nihil that had fallen from their ship. The marauder returned the Jedi's kindness with hate, smashing through Sutmani's Vector cockpit in a final act of malice that killed them both.

TE'AMI

Jedi Knight Te'Ami didn't care much for outside appearances, as evidenced by her plain lightsaber. Its hilt was heavily tarnished with scratches and gouges adorning every part of it and its copper crosspiece. Her disinterest in appearances should not be taken as a lack of caring, for Te'Ami was a compassionate and selfless Jedi Knight. Te'Ami sacrificed herself to save one of the most vital missions following the Great Disaster. She met her end when the Republic mounted a crucial search for the *Legacy Run*'s flight recorder, a device that would offer vital clues to what destroyed the ship. The Nihil in turn fought to destroy the recorder before it could be analyzed. Te'Ami was among the Jedi pilots escorting the Republic retrieval. A Nihil ship launched a missile at the recorder, and Te'Ami forfeited her own life by piloting her Vector into its path before it struck. Her sacrifice led to the discovery that the Nihil were behind the Great Disaster—a turning point in the investigation.

TY YORRICK

The events of the Republic Fair brought the Jedi Order into contact with a Padawan that had veered from her path many years before. Ty Yorrick, as she is now called, is incredibly guarded about her past, and temple records are oddly incomplete. What we do know is that Ty Yorrick had once been a Padawan of the Jedi Order, training for many years.

When the Tholothian strayed from the Order, she came to be a saber for hire, taking odd jobs hunting monsters, extracting individuals from danger, and doing simple bodyguarding for a fee. Rather than following the will of any organization, she believes in flipping varazeen stones to make choices for her. Aside from her droids KL-03 and RO-VR, there is very little to suggest she holds any close relationships.

Try as she might to avoid encounters with the Jedi, the Force eventually led her to cross paths with the Order. Yorrick had traveled to the Valo fair as a paid bodyguard but was apprehended by Elzar Mann when her boss was discovered with an illegal weapon. Her arrest was soon followed by the Nihil attack, allowing her to escape. Mann had confiscated her lightsaber, and getting it back meant that avoiding the Jedi was no longer possible.

As the Nihil attack raged, Ty Yorrick arrived just in time to rescue Elzar Mann from the jaws of a hragscythe that had escaped from the Lonisa City Zoo. Her ability to use the Force proved pivotal as she assisted Mann in bridging minds with a pair of sanvals, dragon-like flying creatures. The Jedi took to the skies with sabers drawn and the sanvals were powerful allies to defend against the Nihil. Her partnership with the Jedi continued after the attack on Valo when Yorrick joined the infiltration of Grizal.

It is yet to be seen if Ty Yorrick returns to her path as a Jedi or if her years away from the Order have severed her connection permanently. The Force clearly has drawn her to these events for a reason, even if her ultimate destiny is unclear.

ELZAR MANN

Elzar Mann might have been one of the greatest Jedi Masters of his generation, but his interest in exploring the Force in unexpected ways sometimes puts him at odds with the teachings of the Jedi Council. Mann is a tinkerer above all else, a Jedi who can find unique solutions to problems, but also pushes boundaries in a way that Jedi typically discourage.

Mann was trained by Jedi Master Quarry and was known as one of the three firebrands along with his peers Avar Kriss and Stellan Gios. Among the three, Mann was the most unconventional, but also the strongest at solving problems with any tool at his disposal. He excelled at sensing deceptions and understanding others, an ability that proved particularly helpful in negotiation and interrogation. It was this skill that led his friend Avar Kriss to call him to assist her investigation into the disaster that befell the *Legacy Run*.

Elzar Mann sees the Force as a bottomless sea that pulls him to the dark depths. He envisions a never-ending ocean and, in it, many curious mysteries. At the time of the Great Disaster, Elzar Mann had been working diligently to achieve the rank of Master, a station that would allow him the freedom to explore the Force he so strongly desired. He attained his goal shortly before the opening of the Republic Fair and was asked to assume leadership of the Valo temple. The newly renovated temple was situated near the site of the upcoming Republic Fair and would soon host dignitaries and Jedi from across the galaxy. It was to be an assignment for Elzar to prove his elevation to Master was well-earned but, instead, became the site for great tragedy for both the Republic and Master Mann personally.

When the Nihil struck at Valo, they savagely targeted the large repulsor platforms that flew above the city. Each celebrated one of the Republic's unique planets but was defenseless against the marauders' air attacks. As one of the largest platforms gave way, it fell toward Lonisa City and threatened the panicked citizens below. Elzar Mann used the Force to hurl the pavilion from its course, but the feat required him to touch the dark side. It was undoubtedly an act of heroism but was achieved using a power that is forbidden to the Jedi. Lives were saved that day, but it is yet to be seen what effect it will have on Mann.

Mann continued to battle the Nihil on Valo, eventually mounting sanval dragons to take to the skies above the burning fair. Like heroes straight out of fantastical holodramas, the Jedi and his new ally Ty Yorrick swept down on the marauders with slashing lightsabers and biting jaws. Jedi below looked upon them in awe, unable to believe their own eyes as Master Elzar Mann and his sanval struck back against the Nihil. Little did they know how tormented he was inside.

After the tragic events of Valo, Elzar Mann took a respite on the moon of Tython to recuperate before returning to Starlight Beacon. His return to the station should have been a turning point as Master Elzar tried to restore balance within himself, but more tragedy was yet to come.

Elzar Mann touches the dark side as he pushes a falling pavilion into Nihil attackers.

CHAPTER 5
GROWING THE ORDER

Recognizing our mistakes and doing
better is the path of a Jedi.

— VERNESTRA RWOH

5

THE *STAR HOPPER*

If experience is a great teacher, then the Jedi Academic Cruiser is the fastest way to teach. The Jedi Order operates these purpose-built academic vessels as a traveling home, school, and transport for more than a dozen students. The bridge is the heart of the ship and offers terminals for all students to get hands-on experience monitoring a situation under the watchful eye of Jedi Masters.

In this time of Republic expansion, the Academic Cruiser is a valuable teaching asset for bringing students to newly opened corners of the galaxy. While our network of temple outposts is growing, a cruiser can perform its duties anywhere with a hyperlane, and every system in the galaxy can become a classroom.

The Academic Cruisers are staffed by one or more instructors who oversee multiple students at a time. It is a temporary learning situation, and most Padawans eventually return to their master's side to complete their training, but it is one that forges lasting friendships among the Padawans who share the journey. Such opportunities are particularly valuable in times when a master must temporarily step away from their apprentice, whether to attend to personal matters or embark on a dangerous mission unfit for a young Padawan.

Each cruiser operates self-sufficiently for months at a time, providing ample opportunity for Padawans to learn about unique perspectives on the Force, visit far-flung temples or ancient sites, and discover what it means to be a Jedi. When students must disembark for an excursion, the cruiser is equipped with speeders and supplies to aid in both exploration and outreach efforts. Students might be called to assist local populations or be ready to intervene to defend others, for even a Padawan is expected to uphold the mission of the Jedi.

One such cruiser, the *Star Hopper*, played a central role in the events following the Great Hyperspace Disaster. Under the watchful eyes of Yoda, Torban Buck, and Kantam Sy, the *Star Hopper*'s voyage of instruction came to an abrupt end when Emergences began to appear across the Outer Rim. The Padawans of the *Star Hopper* were thrust into a very real disaster and a fateful rendezvous with the Nihil for the first time.

YODA, THE TEACHER

Grand Master Yoda's six centuries of service saw him take on a variety of roles within the Order, but teaching is among his most favorite duties. Recently, he has taken a sabbatical from his seat on the High Council for the unlikely role as lead instructor aboard a Padawan training vessel called the *Star Hopper*. The ship's young apprentices may not have appreciated it at the time, but the chance to gain hands-on learning from such an esteemed Jedi Master was truly an honor.

Perhaps in taking the role, Master Yoda was simply following the will of the Force, as his time on the *Star Hopper* led him down a path to uncover an ancient mystery. His rescue mission with the Padawans on Trymant IV led Yoda to discover connections between current day enemies and pieces of Jedi past long forgotten. Though he would embark alone to learn more, the Padawans of the *Star Hopper* carried with them his teachings as they themselves embarked on great adventures.

TORBAN BUCK

The eccentric Chagrian Jedi Master Torban Buck is a towering figure in the Jedi Order. Hiding behind a sizable stature is a compassionate, jovial figure who is far more interested in healing others than doing harm—indeed Master Buck is among the finest medics in the Jedi Order. In fact, his talents as a healer earned him the (self-given) nickname "Buckets of Blood," not because he sought violence, but because he proudly put buckets of blood back into his patients. Nicknames aside, his talents are unquestionable and put to great use after the tragedy on Valo. Master Buck was among the first on the scene to attend to Chancellor Lina Soh's grave injuries that day.

In the time leading up to the Great Hyperspace Disaster, Master Buck served alongside Yoda and Kantam Sy teaching the Padawans of the *Star Hopper*. He was no doubt an unconventional teacher whose zeal led him to organize some unique activities for his students. Amid the ongoing stress of galactic events, Buck organized lighthearted competitions for his students, including races, and stories told over desserts.

OPPOSITE (left to right) Torban Buck, Yoda, and Kantam Sy.

THE *STAR HOPPER* PADAWANS

LULA TALISOLA

Jedi Padawans are exceptional in many ways, but what makes Lula Talisola so extraordinary is her drive to succeed. She eagerly threw herself into her training with a goal to learn every possible skill. It is no secret that she aims to become one of the greatest Jedi ever. Nothing short of that ambitious achievement will satisfy Padawan Talisola. Jedi leadership undeniably sees great potential in Lula, even if at times she questions her own abilities.

Yet, the strength of Lula's connection to the Force was apparent from a young age. Talisola lived in a Naboo orphanage, her abilities still unknown to her caretakers. But when Lula and another orphan found themselves in danger, Master Kantam Sy happened to be nearby. Lula used the Force to save her fellow orphan from a terrible fall, and after witnessing Lula's heroics, Kantam invited Lula into the Jedi Order. It was the beginning of a powerful partnership between teacher and student.

Wisdom beyond her years led her to take up the mantle as the de facto leader of her Padawan peers. It was her accomplishments in the face of adversity that saw her placed in charge of the mission to hunt a young Nihil gang under the leadership of Krix Kamerat. Being placed in charge of a task force at her age was a real honor and typically reserved for Padawans who were growing closer to knighthood.

ZEEN MRALA

One of the most notable youths among the *Star Hopper*'s Padawans is not a Padawan at all. Zeen Mrala was discovered on Trymant IV when the Jedi raced to save the local population from a hyperspace Emergence. Zeen was raised in a religious sect that called itself the Elders of the Path, just one of the many organizations that descended from the Path of the Open Hand more than a century before. These nomadic beings had no permanent home but held a strict view on how the Force should not be used by any individual. Zeen discovered at a young age that she was Force-sensitive but hid her connection from everyone around her. She even kept her abilities a secret from her best friend, Krix.

The disaster on Trymant IV revealed Zeen's powers to the Jedi and her people, leaving her without home nor kin. About the same age as the *Star Hopper*'s Padawans, she was taken in and allowed to live among the Jedi. She formed fast friendships with her fellow teenagers, especially with Lula Talisola with whom she formed a bond that grew beyond mere friendship. As a sort of honorary Padawan, she also earned their respect on numerous missions to foil the Nihil.

Her presence among the Jedi proved key to understanding and thwarting Krix Kamerat as he ascended the Nihil ranks. Like Zeen, he abandoned the Elders of the Path, but chose to follow evil instead of the light. While neither can know where their new paths will ultimately take them, Zeen Mrala's journey will be one surrounded by friends who want to see her reach her full potential.

QORT

This young Aloxian was taken from his people as an infant and left behind on Takodana by pirates. With the help of pirate queen Maz Kanata, Qort's Force abilities were discovered, and he made his

OPPOSITE (clockwise from top) Farzala, Qort, Bibs, Lula, and Zeen.

way to the Jedi Order. Qort continued to speak in his native tongue, which his fellow Padawans learned to accommodate among their group.

His defining physical feature is his traditional vonduun crab mask, an ornament that he has worn for most of his young life. These masks hold great significance to the Aloxians, who credit the coverings for balancing their naturally aggressive nature. Aloxians also believe that when the mask finally shatters from its owner's head, it is a sign that the Aloxian had fully come of age.

Qort remains a favorite of Maz Kanata and her pirate friends, but then again young Qort has a way of endearing himself to almost everyone he meets. Even if they don't understand his language, all who know Qort respect him for his tenderness and loyalty.

FARZALA TARABAL

Like most Padawans, Tarabal was brought to the Order at a young age, and he grew into a kindhearted Jedi Padawan and an endearing storyteller under the guidance of Master Obratuk Glii. Of all of the *Star Hopper* Padawans, it was young Farzala who was most excited for the opportunity to explore the galaxy.

BIBS

The Bravaisian Padawan Bibs is a frequent companion to the *Star Hopper* Padawans, and quick to welcome Zeen to their band. Behind the goggles that protect their sensitive eyes lies an enthusiastic and playful student—some might even say mischievous. Bibs's competitive streak

once led them to replace the fuel in Ram Jomaram's droid with bantha milk!

Though Bibs is short in stature, they don't shy away from a battle when called for. They shared a bridge control station with Lula during their fateful journey to Trymant IV and was among the first

THESE PAGES Qort and Bibs on the defensive.

to notice the Emergence threatening the system. When charging into battle, green lightsaber ablaze, Bibs's trademark yell rings out: "Ay ay ay ay!" Bibs played a vital role in helping the Jedi discover a Nihil encampment on Dol'har Hyde, and they bravely helped in the campaign to bring Krix Kamerat to justice.

PADAWANS DEFEND THE LIGHT

For many of the *Star Hopper* Padawans, their action on Trymant IV was their first real mission in the galaxy. The *Star Hopper* was traveling through hyperspace when Emergences began threatening systems following the Great Disaster. One such Emergence threatened to strike the most populated city in the Trymant system, raining fiery debris from hyperspace onto the helpless population below. The *Star Hopper* was the only Jedi vessel close enough to offer assistance, and

under the leadership of Masters Yoda and Buck, the Padawans raced to the planet surface to save as many as they could.

When they arrived, the Jedi were shocked to discover that molten debris was not the only threat they would face. The Nihil had arrived shortly before the Jedi. The Padawans found another surprise there as well. Living among a commune that refuses to use the Force was Zeen Mrala, a Force-sensitive teen who kept her abilities hidden from those around her. Zeen tapped into her Force powers that day to save her community, but the act was forbidden among her people, and as a result, she was cast out as a heretic. Young Zeen was taken in by the Jedi, an unconventional addition to the *Star Hopper* crew to be sure, but these are unconventional times.

The Padawans found little time for traditional training in the months that followed the Great Disaster. Like so many in the Outer Rim, the Drengir posed a constant threat, as did the Nihil. Their next encounter with the marauders came while training in the Bright Jewel system at the Republic outpost on Ord Mantell. Zeen Mrala discovered the Nihil neophyte Krix Kamerat operating nearby, which led the Padawans to Quantxi, Ord Mantell's notorious junk moon, where they quickly found themselves outnumbered by Nihil raiders. Yet, the Nihil and their blasters were not the most threatening foe they faced that day. The Nihil summoned a monstrous Savrip, towering above the Padawans with its razor-sharp claws. Aided by Master Kantam Sy, Padawans Farzala and Qort distracted the monster long enough to allow the Jedi to escape, proving teamwork can defeat even the most dangerous beasts.

While the Nihil got away as well, the mission led Master Yoda to embark on a mysterious journey in search of something from centuries past. What he was seeking remains unclear, but it seems somehow related to the history of the Nihil. And though they all missed his guidance, the Padawans knew Master Yoda would have never left them behind without good reason.

MISSIONS FOR PEACE

After months of near constant fighting with the Nihil and Drengir, Padawans Farzala and Qort accompanied Master Obratuk Glii as part of a diplomatic envoy to Nal Hutta. In times of peace, a party of Masters would lead such negotiations, but with Jedi resources stretched thin, a single Master with the help of some Padawans would have to suffice. The journey to the homeworld of the Hutts was quickly met with challenges when the ancient Master Obratuk fell into hibernation just as negotiations were to begin.

The Padawans once again found themselves thrust into a high-stakes situation.

No Padawan should be asked to take on such responsibility, especially when dealing with the Hutts. While Skarabda the Hutt sought peace, her rival Jabba aimed to undermine the negotiations. The Padawans fell under attack from all sides as the Hutts took them hostage and the Drengir emerged to sow further chaos.

Farzala mastered his own fear and escaped capture, then turned the tables on the Hutts by using the Force to tame a blixus creature until

OPPOSITE Farzala Tarabal rides a blixus to escape Hutt imprisonment.

Master Glii could emerge from hibernation and return order to the situation. Despite the temporary setbacks, the diplomatic mission was a success, and the Jedi and Hutts agreed to cooperate to defeat their mutual enemy, the Drengir. The alliance proved vital to the eventual defeat of these ancient monsters and was thanks in large part to the resilience of such a young Jedi.

Formed into a special task force to track down the Nihil agent Krix Kamerat, the *Star Hopper* Padawans responded to a Nihil attack on the Jedi temple at Takodana. A single Jedi defender—Sav Malagán—held off the initial exploratory attack. The legendary Jedi warrior had served more than a century before at the Battle of Jedha and more recently maintained a close partnership with the renowned pirate Maz Kanata on Takodana. Malagán's heroics were enough to hold off the first wave, but the Nihil would soon return with more.

The *Star Hopper* crew arrived at Takodana as reinforcements, but they were caught in a blast that rocked the Jedi temple. It had been sabotaged by the Nihil and left Master Malagán incapacitated. The Nihil ships raced to land a killing blow upon the disoriented Jedi when the young Padawan Qort rose up to defend them all. His trademark mask was destroyed in the blast, but his fighting spirit had been unleashed. Qort not only revealed his face but also revealed his true bravery that day.

After months of action against the Nihil, Drengir, and treacherous Hutts, Jedi teachers recognized the need for their young students to find opportunities for joy and relaxation. The Padawans received brief moments of rest back on Starlight Beacon where they could once again live a more normal life as Padawans. Days filled with dueling, study, and comradery were a welcome change for the apprentices who had endured so much.

Master Torban Buck was an enthusiastic proponent of providing lighthearted activities for the Padawans. Their time on Starlight even offered baking competitions and races to test their wit and dexterity. All served to bring the *Star Hopper* Padawans closer together than ever before.

VERNESTRA RWOH AND IMRI CANTAROS

If being accepted into the Jedi Order is an exceedingly rare feat, Vernestra Rwoh's talent and abilities could be described as the rarest of rare. The word *prodigy* has been used to describe the young Mirialan who was knighted at the age of fifteen, making her the youngest to achieve such a rank in the Order in some time. When most of her peers were still Padawans following in the footsteps of their masters, Rwoh was taking on her first mission as a full-fledged Jedi Knight.

That first mission was proof that her early knighthood was no mistake. It began as a simple diplomatic escort mission to Starlight Beacon aboard the luxury liner *Steady Wing* but quickly turned into a battle for survival when the Nihil sabotaged the voyage to upset the delicate political balance between the Republic and the Dalnan delegation on board. The death of Jedi Master Douglas Sunvale left Vernestra the ranking leader of a band of young survivors, including Sunvale's own Padawan, Imri Cantaros.

The disaster on the *Steady Wing* and the survival ordeal on the nearby moon of Wevo put Rwoh's talents on full display, and perhaps pushed

OPPOSITE (left to right) Padawan Imri Cantaros and Knight Vernestra Rwoh.

her even further than she might have imagined. Rwoh had practiced a dueling style modeled after Master Yoda's since she was a youngling, but she evolved her fighting style further when guided by a dream to modify her traditional lightsaber with the ability to form a lightwhip. It is fitting that such a nontraditional Jedi might take up such a nontraditional saber, yet clearly the Force had provided her this unique vision to better prepare for the struggles against both nature and the Nihil during the ordeal on Wevo.

Vernestra Rwoh could not have prepared for her next great trial: taking on her own Padawan when she was but sixteen years old. But during the ordeal on Wevo, Rwoh formed a bond with Padawan Cantaros and proved to be a talented teacher indeed. Imri Cantaros has been described as an extreme empath, having particularly strong talents in sensing the emotions of others. Such a gift can make it hard to maintain balance, as Cantaros discovered when he was captured by the Nihil who killed his master. During this time, Cantaros came dangerously close to the dark side of the Force, feeding off the anger and grief he sensed from a fellow prisoner. Rwoh stepped in to restore balance for the young Jedi, the first of many times she helped Cantaros master his unique gifts, which include the ability to soothe others' emotions.

HYPERSPACE VISIONS

Rwoh's unique abilities extend far beyond her maturity and saber skills. When she was the Padawan of Stellan Gios, Rwoh exhibited the potential for an exceedingly rare ability to see visions while traveling through hyperspace. It was as if she would lose herself while traveling at light speed, her consciousness traveling to new destinations and leaving her with impressions of places she had never been. Ancient texts suggested that the Jedi or Sith had similar abilities long ago, but few, if any, share them today.

Master Gios had long encouraged Vernestra to explore this talent further, but Rwoh had attempted to put them behind her. Indeed, she had not experienced such a vision since becoming a Jedi Knight, at least until her duties led her to a mission in the Berenge Sector. It was a fitting task for a Jedi with a mysterious connection to hyperspace, as she was part of the team chosen to investigate reports of ships being pulled from light speed in that corner of space.

Vernestra's talents led the Jedi to the cause of this disturbance, a space station created by the Nihil. Yet, those who were close to Vernestra whisper that she discovered something far more curious that day. Deep inside the station, dubbed Gravity's Heart by the Nihil, Vernestra found what had been calling to her in her visions. It was Mari San Tekka, somehow kept alive for over a century after her disappearance.

Some say that it was no coincidence that when Mari began prospecting with her family at the age of six, the family began having unprecedented success. Some suggest that Mari had unique abilities to see paths through hyperspace that computers and droids could not.

When the young Mari was kidnapped, she was thought to be never seen again. Her rediscovery aboard the Gravity's Heart led to many questions. How did she survive so long? Why did the Nihil keep her prisoner in a medical capsule? The

OPPOSITE Vernestra's visions are rare among Jedi.

Order may never fully answer these questions, as Vernestra was the last to see her. Mari San Tekka died that day at more than one hundred years old, and Gravity's Heart was destroyed.

Some Republic strategists believed that the destruction of Gravity's Heart was a sign that the Nihil threat was coming to a close. They assumed that the ragtag space station was a last-ditch effort by the raiders to disrupt travel in the Outer Rim, much like Nihil had done by destroying the *Legacy Run*. Many saw these two separate events as evidence that the Nihil were simply attempting to sow chaos and halt progress across the hyperspace lanes. Furthermore, most believed that the death of Mari San Tekka was a sign that the Nihil's supremacy across the hyperlanes had come to an end.

How wrong they were. The Gravity's Heart was an impressive advancement of Nihil technology but it was not the endgame.

ADY SUN'ZEE AND THE JEDI TEMPLE OF BATUU

Temple postings are common for a Padawan, but that does not mean that they are without their dangers. The temple on Batuu was lost to the Order and nearly took with it a Padawan named Ady Sun'Zee. Her ordeal began when her master, Sylwin, delivered an ancient Sith runestone to the research temple on Batuu. Sylwin followed all Jedi protocol and quickly reported the findings to Coruscant for further analysis. But the runestone had a powerful connection to the dark side of the Force, and it quickly overwhelmed the Jedi stationed on Batuu. Sylwin fell attempting to combat its energies, but her act of selflessness allowed Ady to activate a

distress beacon to the Jedi Council on Coruscant.

Given Batuu's remote location, Grand Master Yoda arrived days later to find Ady herself corrupted and confused by the darkness that had overtaken the temple. The power of the runestone was so strong that Yoda declared the temple was lost. Together, Master Yoda and Padawan Sun'Zee struggled to contain the relic's dark-side energy, eventually combining their strength to seal it away. Ady hid the keys to the temple somewhere on Batuu, should the Force ever require the Jedi to return.

Though Ady had been touched by the dark side, her bravery in sealing the darkness inside the temple was more than proof that her connection to the light had been restored.

The temple on Batuu was a fine example of a Jedi research outpost, and its loss was unfortunate. The temple's balconies provided magnificent views of the planet's ancient spires and were a favorite of the Jedi who meditated there. There has been some debate among the Jedi in the wake of the temple's closure as to why the Sith relic caused so much destruction.

Some believe that the runestone drew upon the powerful energy of the Force that flows on Batuu. The relic was deemed safe before it came to the planet, but the concentration of the Force found here provided enough power to activate the runestone's sinister energies. Proponents of this theory point to the corruption of hordes of local demlins and the deaths of the outpost Jedi to support their theory. If true, it makes the loss of the Batuu temple even more unfortunate. Losing such a sacred site was not taken lightly by the Order.

OPPOSITE The rocky spires of Batuu tower over Ady Sun'Zee.

CHAPTER 6
IN DEFENSE OF LIGHT

Am I ready? No. Will I ever be ready?

Same answer—but I'm gonna try.

— KEEVE TRENNIS

THE JEDI AS PEACEKEEPERS

The life of a Jedi is to follow a unique path guided by the Force. Jedi seek to maintain balance in all things, as they forge an ever-deeper connection to both the cosmic and living energies that surround us all. While a Jedi should always seek to find knowledge and harmony, there are times when a Jedi must step in as the guardians of justice to defend themselves and others.

Wars of centuries past are but a fading memory today. The Sith, long held as the greatest threat to the Jedi, have not been seen in centuries. These past decades have been some of the most peaceful and prosperous in all of known galactic history, but even still, the Jedi are called upon to help as peacekeepers for a variety of reasons.

Despite a Jedi's greatest efforts, peace is not always possible, so all are trained to defend themselves from a young age. Through the Force, a Jedi can achieve feats others cannot, making them capable warriors in the fight against evil. The Jedi's greatest tool in these situations is often the lightsaber, and through centuries of service, it has become the icon of our Order in the eyes of outsiders throughout the galaxy. There are some who lament this fact, believing that the Jedi have strayed too far by taking up arms too frequently. Others take a more pragmatic view. They believe that a Jedi must use their powers for good, even if it means that we come to be seen as guardians first and foremost.

While peacekeeping has become a frequent mission for Jedi throughout the frontier, the Order is not an army. Widespread dangers such as the Nihil and Drengir have stretched our ranks thin. Our Order is being tested in a way that it has not

been challenged for some time. Many secretly wonder, Can we rise to meet these challenges?

ELEGANT WEAPONS

Lightsabers are far more than just a weapon. They are a symbol of the focus and training a Jedi must undertake. The saber is a tool of last resort, but when they must be wielded, they are designed to do only as much harm as absolutely needed. They are uniquely fit to the Jedi who wield them because the kyber crystal inside chooses its wielder. The hilts are often a reflection of each Jedi's values, style, and background. For instance, duelists who prefer more aggressive tactics might choose a saber with multiple blades. Species with multiple limbs often choose to carry two or more matching sabers, while diminutive Jedi might craft smaller hilts to match their small stature. This time of prosperity and expansion has led to perhaps the widest array of lightsaber designs ever found among the Jedi. Lightsabers of the age are notable for their ornamental embellishments, while remaining as effective as those of eras past. In fact, some Jedi choose to tinker with more experimental designs as they embark deeper on their personal journey to understand the Force.

Master Avar Kriss wields a green-bladed saber noted for its elegant and powerful design. Its prominent crossguard sits atop a grip inlaid with bright-green seastone running through length of the hilt.

OPPOSITE Jedi Master Obratuk Glii, who is over one thousand years old, wields sabers created in memory of his former Padawans.

Master Stellan Gios wielded one of the most intricately designed lightsabers in the Order. In addition to a brilliant blue primary blade, the hilt emits dual crossguard blades thanks to a vented emitter. The pair of quillons point forward for ease of storage but extend outward to cap the crossguard blades when ignited.

Padawan Burryaga's lightsaber is an ever-present reminder of the natural wonders of his homeworld, Kashyyyk. The hilt is fashioned from the amber of a white wroshyr tree, and it is wrapped in the leather of a tach, a primate native to the planet. This hilt is topped with a crosspiece plated in pure electrum. Burryaga's blue-bladed saber was specially designed to be comfortable for a towering Wookiee and is among the longest in the Order.

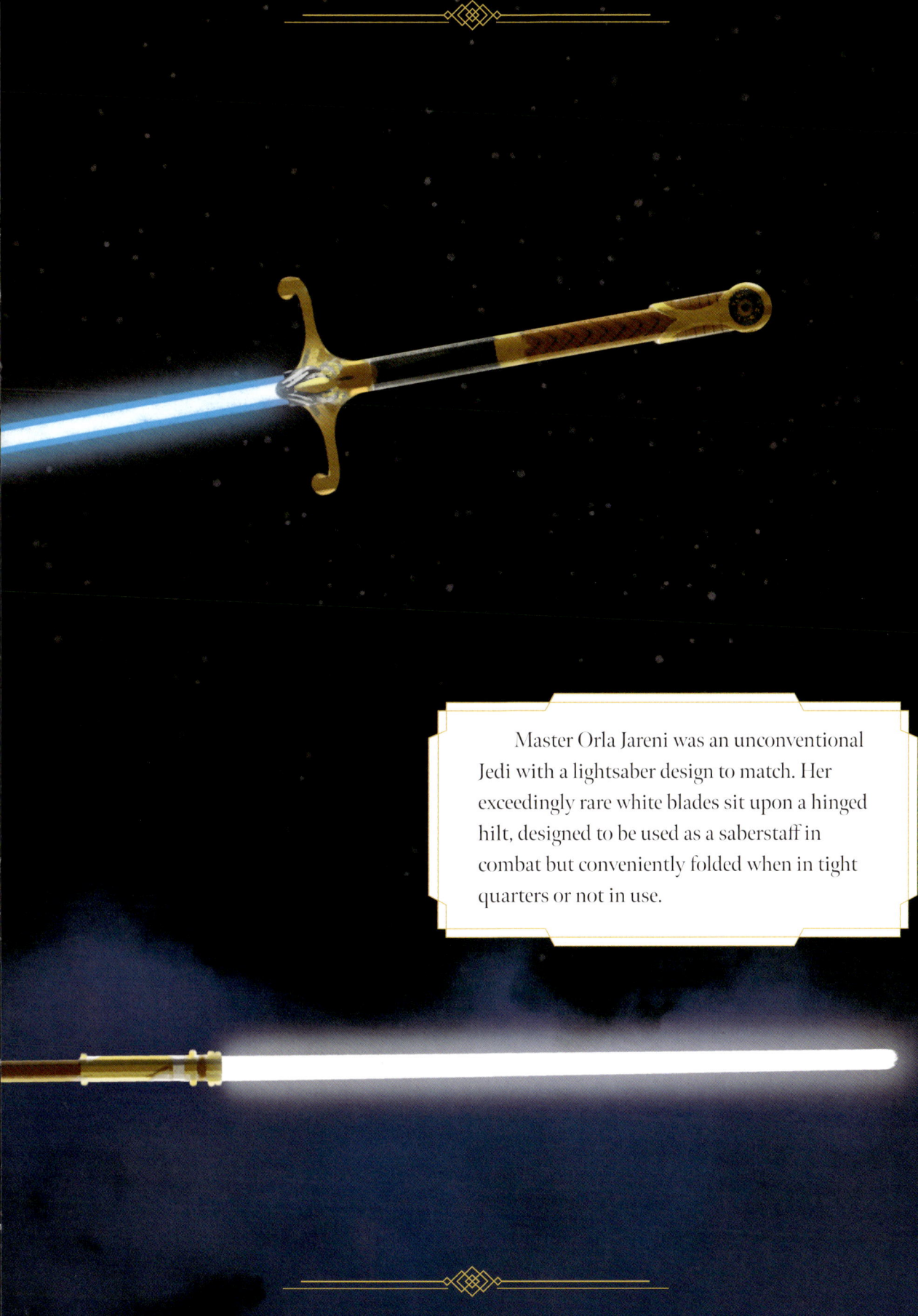

Master Orla Jareni was an unconventional Jedi with a lightsaber design to match. Her exceedingly rare white blades sit upon a hinged hilt, designed to be used as a saberstaff in combat but conveniently folded when in tight quarters or not in use.

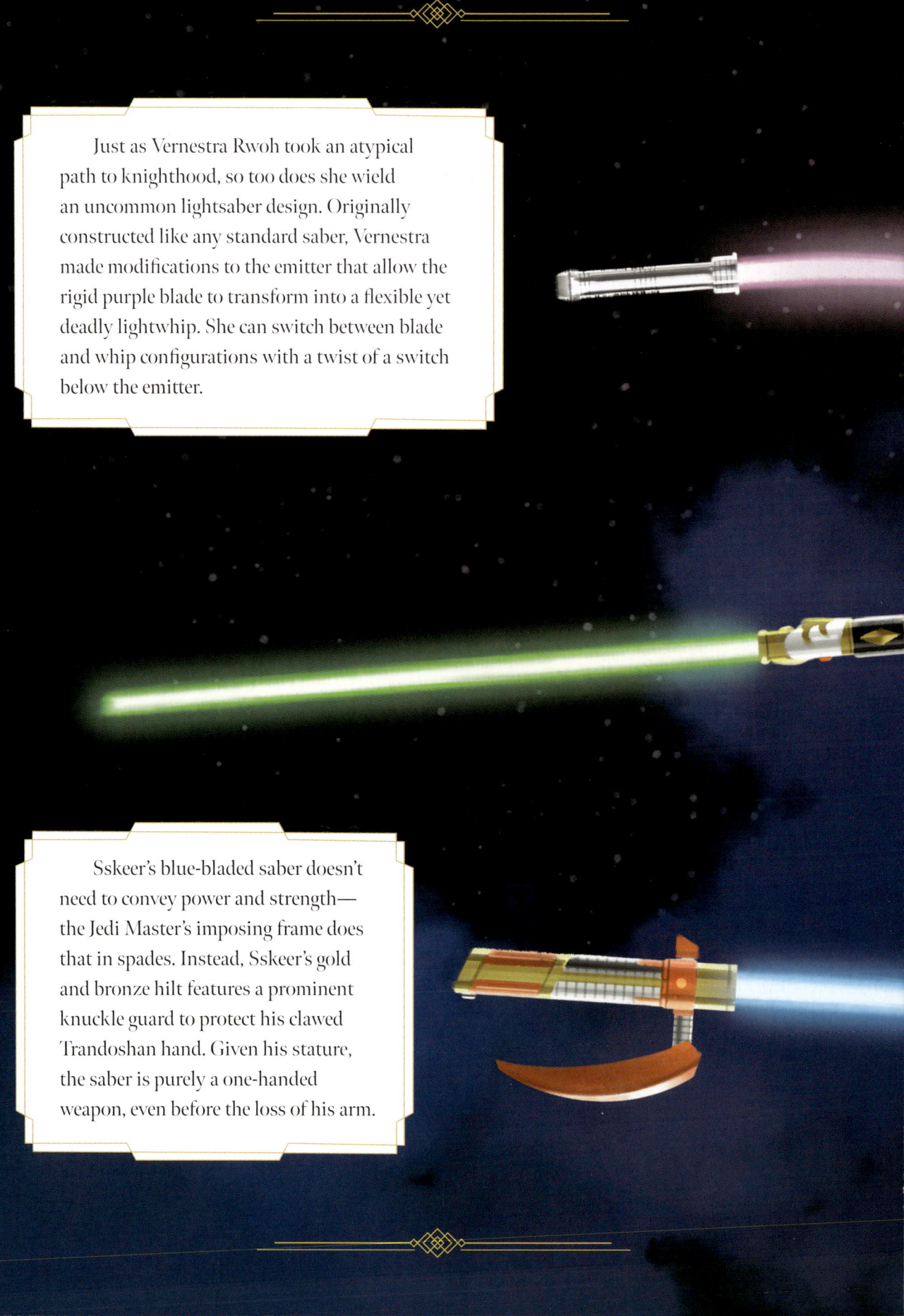

Just as Vernestra Rwoh took an atypical path to knighthood, so too does she wield an uncommon lightsaber design. Originally constructed like any standard saber, Vernestra made modifications to the emitter that allow the rigid purple blade to transform into a flexible yet deadly lightwhip. She can switch between blade and whip configurations with a twist of a switch below the emitter.

Sskeer's blue-bladed saber doesn't need to convey power and strength—the Jedi Master's imposing frame does that in spades. Instead, Sskeer's gold and bronze hilt features a prominent knuckle guard to protect his clawed Trandoshan hand. Given his stature, the saber is purely a one-handed weapon, even before the loss of his arm.

Knight Keeve Trennis fashioned two identical green-bladed lightsabers. Each saber features an endcap connector that allows her to join the two sabers into one saberstaff. Trennis is a capable fighter in any configuration, switching between dual sabers and staff depending on the situation.

REATH SILAS

Though apprenticed to one of the Order's finest masters, and having access to the Grand Temple on Coruscant's vast resources, nothing could have prepared Padawan Reath Silas for the events that followed the Great Disaster. Padawan Silas would be the first to admit that he was more comfortable in the archives than in the field, and thanks to his master's time serving on the Jedi Council, his years as a Padawan played to his preferences. Limited travel meant limitless time studying languages, memorizing machine schematics, and analyzing frameworks. Reath was a hard worker who would pour his energies into his academic projects, many of which were self-assigned. His natural abilities were not exceptional, but his hard work led his master to believe that his future held great potential.

His master, Jora Malli, believed Silas would benefit from a posting to the frontier and to Starlight Beacon. It would be a difficult change for Reath to leave his comfort zone, surrounded by the vast resources held by the Jedi on Coruscant, but necessary for him to grow as he approached the age when he might take his trials for knighthood. Silas was to meet his master in time for the dedication of Starlight Beacon, but his travels were put to a halt when the Great Disaster at Hetzal struck and the resulting hyperspace anomalies left him stranded in deep space with fellow Jedi Dez Rydan, Orla Jareni, and Cohmac Vitus. The four Jedi took refuge on an ancient Amaxine space station, a structure built before recorded history by a vanished alien culture but was soon to be the site of one of the first engagements with two powerful foes: the Nihil and the Drengir.

Reath proved himself to be a capable guardian against the Drengir at the Amaxine station, but he had little time to recuperate from the stress of his first major combat mission. Amid this challenge, Reath learned that his own master had become one with the Force at the Battle of Kur. For a time, he wondered if he belonged with the Jedi Order at all but ultimately chose to continue his training under the tutelage of Cohmac Vitus, having formed a bond during the events on the Amaxine station.

In the months that followed, Reath endured the trauma of watching a culture threaten to destroy itself on Genetia, was taken hostage multiple times, battled the Drengir on Mulita, and was a prisoner of the Nihil on the terrifying space station Gravity's Heart. Reath and Master Cohmac once again answered the call to fight the Nihil when the raiders attempted a bold plot to infiltrate one of the Republic's most critical shipyards on Corellia. The fighting there shook all involved to their core and tested more experienced Masters, yet Reath Silas proved that in little more than a year, he had grown from a sheltered Padawan to a Jedi Knight, forged by trial after trial. It is yet to be seen how such a challenging path might shape the young Jedi's outlook, but Reath's knighthood was undoubtedly earned through great struggle and hardship.

DEZ RYDAN

As if the exact opposite of Reath Silas, Dez Rydan was a former Padawan of Jora Malli who craved endless adventure. Quick to action and brave to a fault, Dez Rydan could have been mistaken for the hero of a holodrama. Soon after reaching knighthood, Dez embraced every mission he was given by the Council, and perhaps a few that weren't. Word spread quickly throughout the Order of his exploits on Zeitooine and Christophsis, though he usually let his saber skills do most of his talking.

Dez Rydan was among the Jedi traveling to Starlight Beacon and marooned on the Amaxine station. While exploring its ancient passageways, Dez was transported to a mysterious world and taken captive by the Drengir. The murderous plants poisoned his mind, and he nearly killed Reath Silas, who was attempting to rescue him. The events of his capture were so traumatic that the mission on the Amaxine station became his last. Dez Rydan decided to contemplate his relationship with the Force, and set aside his adventurous ways by taking the Barash Vow. His future lies on one of the contemplation worlds in long-term meditation.

BELOW Reath Silas (left) defends against Dez Rydan (right) who is under the influence of the Drengir.

OPPOSITE The ancient Amaxine space station.

COHMAC VITUS

As one of the Order's most well-regarded scholars, Cohmac Vitus was looking forward to his posting at Starlight Beacon to expand his studies of folklore. The new hub on the frontier was to offer endless opportunities to study new cultures, but Nihil and Drengir attacks left little time for research. Instead, Vitus's abilities as a negotiator and guardian were regularly tested.

As he typically worked alone in his studies, Vitus had not expected to take a Padawan so soon when the events of the Amaxine station led him to Reath Silas. Perhaps Silas's sudden loss of his master was a familiar challenge to Vitus, who had himself dealt with Master Simmix's death during the Eiram-E'ronoh hostage crisis twenty-five years earlier. Vitus and Silas proved to be a formidable Master-Padawan duo, as their posting at Starlight Beacon saw them frequently deployed to combat zones.

His scholarly background led Cohmac to Genetia after the Great Disaster. Genetia's inhabitants were famously prone to wide-ranging emotion, a fact that had seen the culture spiraling toward civil war. Vitus led a mission to save precious relics and archives from destruction on behalf of the Republic. They would be carefully chosen, catalogued, and eventually returned when the troubles had passed. For a great folklorist and his scholarly Padawan, it was a fitting mission to distract from many more dangerous postings.

Like many Jedi, Cohmac Vitus felt strong emotion and regularly took time to meditate to rebalance himself in challenging situations. The events that followed the Great Disaster constantly tested his resolve. Perhaps it was the flurry of disasters and tragedies that led Master Vitus to his breaking point at Corellia. There, he fought valiantly against overwhelming numbers of Nihil, but wider events led him to question his path. After knighting his Padawan, Cohmac Vitus handed over his lightsaber and declared that he was leaving the Order.

ORLA JARENI

Jedi Knight Orla Jareni was an Umbaran with sharp features and an even sharper wit. Humility, a virtue of any great Jedi, does not come naturally to her. Some might say that her many talents were to blame, and it is undeniable that she was quick to master new skills. Her connection to the Force was instinctive, some might even say primal. She did not fall into the trap of holding a rigid and inflexible view of the Force, a fault that ensnared so many Jedi over the centuries. Jareni was excellent at improvisation and proved time and again that she was willing to set aside emotion and let the Force guide her path.

Shortly before the Great Disaster, Orla Jareni declared herself a Wayseeker. The life of a Wayseeker is starkly different from most Jedi Knights. These self-directed Jedi unquestionably let the Force guide their path, even if that means going outside of the Jedi Order's regulations, traditions, and oversight. They do not leave the Order, but they also don't work at its behest. After the Great Disaster, the Force led Jareni to cross paths with Keeve Trennis in a battle against the Nihil. Jareni went on to serve in the Jedi's battles

OPPOSITE (left to right) Cohmac Vitus and Orla Jareni.

with the Drengir, Nihil, and eventually followed the Force to Starlight Beacon.

As Padawans, Jareni and Vitus accompanied their masters to investigate the kidnapping of royals from Eiram and E'ronoh, two frontier planets that had been locked in a cold war for a century. The two planets sat at the edge of a spacelane that could prove valuable to galactic commerce if not for the two royal families refusing to cooperate. The Hutts hired a local crime organization to capture a member from each royal family, finally prompting both sides to call the Jedi for aid. The mission was deemed a success because Jedi intervention led to an improvement in relations between Eiram and E'ronoh, but the death of Vitus's master weighed on him for decades to come. Similarly, Jareni's experience during the hostage crisis led her to question whether she should serve at the will of the Council, eventually leading her to take up her life as a Wayseeker.

DARK RELICS

Expansion into the Outer Rim brought the Jedi into contact with new mysteries and foes long forgotten. Jedi Reath Silas, Dez Rydan, Orla Jareni, and Cohmac Vitus were aboard a civilian vessel stranded during the Great Hyperspace Disaster when they took refuge in an ancient space station built long ago by a race known as the Amaxine. Droids tended to an arboretum full of living plants, and among the sprawling foliage, the Jedi discovered four mysterious idols.

The station radiated with a feeling of darkness. The Jedi each sensed cold energies, and young Padawan Silas experienced a vision of being attacked. After a brief examination, the Jedi understandably concluded that the darkness they felt on the station was emanating from the statues. For a time, they considered abandoning them entirely but feared that they might cause harm to others who might stumble upon the relics. Destroying them risked unleashing dark energy, so it was decided that the Jedi should transport the statues back to the Grand Temple on Coruscant for further analysis.

In the Shrine in the Depths of the Grand Temple on Coruscant, the Jedi Council gathered a group of powerful Masters to study these ancient artifacts. They joined their minds together in the Force, but when they gathered their focus to look upon the idols, there was no darkness at all.

During the ritual, the Jedi realized a grave mistake. The idols were not causing the darkness on the Amaxine station—they had been holding it back.

Masters Jareni and Cohmac, along with Padawan Silas, attempted to return the idols to the station, but they were too late. There, they discovered the true source of the dark energies: a sentient species of plants known as the Drengir. The Jedi barely escaped their first confrontation

with the carnivorous plants, killing those that occupied the station by venting it into space. The Jedi survived, but their victory was fleeting.

Our archivists now believe that the Amaxines built the ancient space station long ago to fight the Drengir, only to have their enemy take the station. Sometime later, the Sith forged an alliance with the carnivorous plants, then later betrayed their allies and sealed them away using the four idols. The removal of the statues, however temporary, freed the Drengir root-mind and led to the reemergence of the Drengir across thousands of Outer Rim worlds.

THESE PAGES Four statues with a connection to the dark side bound the Drengir root-mind to the Amaxine station.

SSKEER

The Trandoshan Jedi Master Sskeer served in the years before the Great Disaster as the capable and loyal second-in-command to Council member Jora Malli aboard the starship *Ataraxia*. He flew with her at the Battle of Kur and lost his arm to the Nihil's vicious attack. A Trandoshan's arm regrows with time, but the loss of Master Malli was permanent, and over the months that followed, Master Sskeer experienced far more than just physical trauma.

The plants encountered on the Amaxine space station were not to be the last. Master Sskeer was among the Jedi on Sedri Minor when the Drengir reemerged across the galaxy. The carnivorous plants seemed to be without weakness, but Master Sskeer allowed himself to be infested by the plants to learn the true nature of the enemy. He joined with their root-mind and turned the creatures back, temporarily saving the Jedi, but he nearly lost himself in the process. While he is no longer under the control of the Drengir, those who know him best say that Master Sskeer was never himself again. His connection to the Force is closing because the Jedi Master suffers from Magrak Syndrome, a condition that slowly takes hold in a Trandoshan's brain and allows base urges of aggression, rage, and fury to take over.

KEEVE TRENNIS

Knight Keeve Trennis's assignment to Starlight Beacon placed her at the center of the Republic's battle with both the Drengir and the Nihil. She was knighted just weeks before the Great Hyperspace Disaster, after serving as apprentice to Master Sskeer. She remained with her former master on Sedri Minor where Trennis was among the first to encounter the deadly Drengir. There, she watched firsthand as her master struggled to control his infection, and eventually, she allowed herself to be infected to reach him.

By connecting with the oldest and greatest of the Drengir, Keeve Trennis successfully learned of the root-world where the Great Progenitor hid. It was a selfless act that helped turn the tide against the unstoppable Drengir threat, but came at a great personal cost. Trennis struggled with a lingering connection to dark energies but eventually regained her balance. At Mulita, she stood bravely against the Great Progenitor and reclaimed her independence from the root-mind's control.

Even after her struggles with the Drengir, Trennis remains steadfast in her dedication to the Jedi cause in the Outer Rim. She volunteered for an undercover mission to infiltrate the Nihil and capture the ruthless Tempest Runner Lourna Dee. At the time, the Jedi believed they had nearly defeated the Nihil, but what Keeve discovered during her mission was far more terrifying than anything she had encountered with the Drengir. The Nihil were in control of the mysterious creature that attacked on Grizal, and they could seemingly command it against Force-users. Keeve was lucky to survive the encounter, but soon many others would not be so fortunate.

OPPOSITE Keeve Trennis and Sskeer come face-to-face with a Drengir.

THE DRENGIR

The Drengir discovered on the Amaxine station were just the first of many that threatened the Outer Rim. They were not simply bloodthirsty animals but rather towering, sentient plants— intelligent beings who could speak, form alliances, and outsmart their prey. The vicious plants viewed all living flesh as food, what they called "meat," to be consumed. While the Drengir did not wield the Force, there is no question that they had a strong connection to the dark side.

The Drengir were lying dormant for centuries. When they emerged, they appeared by the thousands, seemingly all at once. As they ravaged the frontier, rumors and speculation about their spread abound. Most now believe that Drengir spores had been dormant underground, and when the Great Progenitor was released on the Amaxine station, the rest of the Drengir awoke.

The flurry of activity as the Republic expanded in the frontier merely gave them additional opportunities to infest new planets. The Jedi were overwhelmed with requests for help at a time when our ranks were already spread thin by the Emergences and the remaining Nihil.

Tales of Jedi gallantry sprung forth to battle, but for every victory, it felt as if the Republic was dealt many more losses. The Drengir could reproduce faster than they could be defeated, leaving the Jedi to search for a new way to halt their advance. Sacrifices by Jedi Sskeer and Keeve Trennis furthered our understanding of the Drengir composition and led to a breakthrough in strategy. The millions of individual Drengir were controlled by a single root-mind, known as the Great Progenitor. This ancient and evil being directed all of the Drengir across the Outer Rim, and her defeat would mean a swift victory. Bold action by Jedi Keeve Trennis led the Jedi to Mulita in Wild Space for one ultimate confrontation.

LILY TORA-ASI

In the wake of the Great Disaster, the Order was establishing a new Jedi temple on the fertile planet of Banchii, a world that welcomed refugees from the hyperspace Emergences. Among the Jedi overseeing the temple construction was Lily Tora-Asi, a young Knight and former Padawan of the Wookiee Master Arkoff. Lily is a Jedi who held firm to her principles, but her strong convictions could also be interpreted as rigidity. Even after she was knighted, Master Arkoff regularly reminded her to be more flexible in her worldview. Training younglings on Banchii and mentoring her own Padawan, Keerin Fionn, proved to be a valuable teaching experience for Lily, as she worked to see the galaxy through others' eyes.

Though Lily Tora-Asi continues to grow as a Jedi, her saber skills are unquestionable. Her dual sabers have distinctive handguards, and her proficiency with them was on display when a mutated Drengir emerged to attack Banchii's local farmers. These powerful new Drengir could seemingly turn their victims into wood. When cut down, these Drengir would multiply, calling on Lily

to find more creative means to combat them. These new Drengir puzzled the Jedi, as they continued to attack even after the Great Progenitor was defeated. Lily performed so admirably against this new threat that she was to lead the investigation of the perplexing new development as the leader of the Banchii temple.

Lily Tora-Asi's resilience and newfound flexibility served her well when the Nihil later struck at Banchii. The marauders overwhelmed the Jedi defenders, and the temple was lost. Even after watching her own Padawan fall to a Nihil blade, Lily remained steadfast in her commitment to protect others. As the other Jedi recalled to safety, Lily stayed behind to protect the local population.

ABOVE Lily Tora-Asi and Master Arkoff face a distinctive Drengir on Banchii.

THE HUTT ALLIANCE

During the darkest days of the battle against the Drengir, the Jedi on the front lines were faced with many difficult circumstances. So many lives were at stake, and the line between friend and foe could become blurred. Faced with a new enemy that they barely understood, the Jedi led by Avar Kriss on Sedri Minor began working with factions of the Hutt cartel to fight back. Such an alliance immediately sparked concern among the Jedi Council who sat safely in their tower on Coruscant. But Kriss had seen firsthand the power of the Drengir, and she knew that in such desperate times, the Jedi could not be rigid in choosing their allies.

The partnership was initially focused on turning the tide against the Drengir, yet some hoped that the cooperation could lead to greater peace and a new treaty with Nal Hutta. That is, if the Hutts could be trusted.

The Hutt alliance began with a rocky start. Initial interactions on Sedri Minor broke out into conflict between the Jedi and the cartel led by Myarga the Hutt. Quickly, the two factions realized that the greater threat was the Drengir, and Myarga called for her rancor-mounted warriors to stand with the Jedi to repel the carnivorous plants.

Myarga the Hutt fought with a zeal and confidence rarely found among the Jedi Order. She wore the skulls of her past foes upon her battle armor while charging into the fight atop her war dais. With beam gauntlets blaring, an army of enforcers, and flanked by battle rancors bred for fighting, she was emboldened by the chaos of battle. Unlikely as they were, Avar Kriss and Myarga became the galaxy's greatest hope to repel the Drengir scourge.

The Hutts proved to be vital allies in the months ahead. Though the cartel was typically more interested in profits, attacks by the Drengir in Hutt space gave them a reason to fight back. With the Jedi at their side to provide balance against their more destructive urges, the Hutts helped hold back the Drengir threat until a breakthrough could be made.

THESE PAGES Myarga leads Avar Kriss, Ceret, and Terec into battle on Daivak.

FATE OF THE DRENGIR

Keeve Trennis's harrowing discovery of the Drengir root-world on Mulita proved to be the most vital breakthrough of the entire Drengir campaign. Marshal Kriss rallied all available Jedi to her side for their final stand against the Great Progenitor. With the Hutts at their side, the Jedi fought a protracted advance upon the forest home of the Drengir root-mind. The Drengir fought vigorously to defend their leader, as she controlled the minds of every Drengir at that battle.

In the end, it was Jedi bravery and ingenuity that turned the tide. Centuries before, the Sith used the dark side to sever the root-mind and the Great Progenitor behind idols. The Jedi in turn used the light side of the Force to perform a similar act. Reaching out with the Force, the Jedi worked in unison to sever her bond with the rest of the Drengir. Once the bond was broken, the Jedi activated their stasis fields to hold her back permanently. The Drengir outside of the field crumpled into a pile of brush.

Just as quickly as it began, the Jedi-Hutt alliance fell apart. With the root-mind trapped, Myarga demanded vengeance. Nothing short of the Great Progenitor's complete destruction would satisfy the Hutts after months of battle. Master Kriss refused to let them go any further, insisting that the Jedi are sworn to protect life, however destructive. The Hutts departed and icy relations soon followed just as they had before the Drengir crisis. The Drengir root-mind was to be held permanently in the Bogan Vault on Starlight Beacon under the watchful eye of the Jedi Order.

The Jedi believed this to be the end of the Drengir threat, but some rare reemergences have challenged that assumption. Lily Tora-Asi's mutated Drengir found on Banchii was the first but not the only discovery of a unique Drengir. Kashyyyk suffered a mysterious attack by a Drengir variant during the preparations for Life Day. While most celebrate the victory on Mulita, the troubling developments on Banchii and Kashyyyk point

to a worrying set of mutations that could allow Drengir to reemerge even without the root-mind to coordinate their attacks.

BELOW The Jedi work in unison to subdue the Great Progenitor.

CERET & TEREC

While it can be said that all Jedi share a bond, none share quite so literal a connection as the Kotabi Jedi Knights Ceret and Terec. Even before the conflict with the Nihil and Drengir, the two had grown legendary among the Order for their unique abilities. While they are of two bodies, each with their own green lightsaber, they share a single mind. Each sees, hears, feels, and thinks with the other, even so far as to feel the physical pain of their sibling. They look virtually identical, making it hard to tell one from the other. However, it seems they are rarely apart, one always nearby to finish the other's sentence. Watching the twins in a lightsaber duel is particularly fascinating, as they play out much like playing dejarik against oneself: One always knows the other's next move.

Their shared mind proved to be a valuable asset to the Jedi in their hunt for the Nihil. Infiltrating the Nihil ranks alongside Keeve Trennis, the twins could provide a valuable communication link while undercover. A commlink would risk being discovered by the Nihil, so the Jedi infiltration team relied on the twins' inseparable bond to communicate. Once they had infiltrated the Nihil Tempest, one twin could signal to the other their location. This rare bond allowed the Jedi to get the jump on the Nihil who had become so skilled at evading capture.

The twins' abilities were also a liability in other situations. Their shared sense of physical pain meant that an injury to one twin could disable the other. On Sedri Minor, Ceret was captured and infested by the Drengir, then a largely unknown threat. Though Ceret was incapacitated, their bond-twin Terec was also inflicted by the infestation and attacked their fellow Jedi. It was a harrowing experience for the twins, and once the infestation was removed, the two swore never to be apart again. If only war were so simple.

During the infiltration of the Nihil Tempest, Jedi Trennis and Terec were confronted by a mysterious weapon. Jedi Trennis suffered a debilitating sense of terror but was not physically harmed. Terec was not so fortunate. They, too, were struck by the sensation of falling into a void, empty and without the Force. Many parsecs away in deep space, Ceret suffered the same way. Mentally, they had lost their connection to the Force. Physically, their bodies became partially calcified, and their skin hardened into a gray crust. The Jedi raced to the scene of the attack, but it was not in time to save the twins or understand what had caused such trauma.

Once again, the twins were returned to each other's side, but it was not how any of us could have planned. When the Nihil escaped, the paralyzed twins were returned to Starlight Beacon in a self-imposed hibernation trance without the ability to move or communicate. Their infliction remains a mystery to the Jedi's best healers but underscores the terrible cost paid by the Order in our struggle against the Nihil.

OPPOSITE (left to right) Terec and Ceret.

MYSTERIOUS FOES

The suffering experienced by Ceret and Terec do not appear to be unique cases. Prior to their affliction, the Jedi experienced other mysterious disturbances during their battles against the Nihil.

The Battle of Grizal was considered a great success by military standards. After the attack on Valo, the Jedi tricked a captive into leading them directly to a large Nihil camp. With the element of surprise on their side, as well as the power of the Force, the Jedi-led contingent quickly disarmed and captured a large portion of the Nihil cell. But in the midst of the battle, three noted Jedi were struck with unexplained ailments.

Master Elzar Mann was piloting a Vector near a large Nihil flagship when he was suddenly struck by a terrifying vision. The experience was so painful that he lost control of himself and his Vector, crashing into the surface below. Upon being rescued, Elzar spoke of an unavoidable dread.

Padawan Bell Zettifar saw something that was hard to describe but reported the sensation of falling and hearing a voice screaming his name. In the mist, he felt the presence of a terrible beast with an insatiable hunger running and chasing him. His after-action reports mention a darkness with hundreds of teeth.

Bell Zettifar survived that day, but was incapacitated by fear from what he had seen. As the rain poured down on the battlefield, and as Jedi elsewhere routed the Nihil defenders, Zettifar had to be helped off the battlefield by Indeera Stokes.

Zettifar's former master, Loden Greatstorm, faced a far worse fate. The Twi'lek master had faced months of torture as a Nihil captive and had only just escaped from their flagship. After a brief reunion with Bell was interrupted, Loden Greatstorm was turned into a gray husk. This powerful Jedi Master had the Force seemingly drained from his body, which then turned to a pile of dust in the Grizal rain.

After falling victim to the mysterious weapon while tracking the Nihil Tempest Runner Lourna Dee, Jedi Keeve Trennis offered up her own description of the mystery. She described a giant monster with prominent claws, large enough to tower over a standard human.

Every new encounter with this being, whatever it may be, only led to more questions. Most troubling of all, the husking that occurred on both Ceret and Terec suggests that the affliction has the power to move through the Force.

EMERICK CAPHTOR

Noted for his calm demeanor and focus, Master Emerick Caphtor is a noted investigator dispatched by the Jedi Council to solve its most curious puzzles. His direct style allows Emerick to get straight to the truth on most topics and his intuition was well guided by the Force. With the help of his droid Cuetwo, there is rarely a mystery that he cannot unravel. But the mystery surrounding the events on Grizal proved to be his toughest ever.

Initial analysis of Greatstorm's remains offered little to go by. The most curious finding was that there was no evidence of midi-chlorians among the dust and nothing to suggest it was even Master Greatstorm. Caphtor's investigation led to the

OPPOSITE Bell Zettifar comes
into contact with the Nameless.

discovery of a rogue Nihil attempting to sell a weapon on the black market and a Nihil spy high in the Republic government, but few clues as to what had struck at Grizal.

Throughout the investigation, the most curious phenomenon happened for those most close to the mystery. Both Caphtor and Master Stellan Gios were drawn to an old nursery rhyme that originated on the planet Dalna. It went like this:

It was an ominous sign of what was to come, for these strange afflictions were not to be the last.

shrii ka rai ka rai

we're coming to take you away.

they'll do what they can . . .

they'll do what they must . . .

. . . but when they find you all you'll be is dust.

ABOVE A nursery rhyme familiar to Stellan Gios and Emerick Caphtor, mysteriously connected to the monsters threatening the Jedi.

OPPOSITE Emerick Caphtor, Jedi investigator, tasked with discovering the cause of recent mysterious attacks.

JEDI OF THE DALNA TEMPLE

In the aftermath of a war a century and a half ago, the Jedi constructed a temple on Dalna to keep a foothold on the battle-ravaged planet. After all that time, the citizens of Dalna remained suspicious of the Jedi and the Republic, tolerating the former but always keeping them at a safe distance. Where once was great conflict now was a peaceful outpost, better known for providing refuge for tooka cats than for excitement and adventure. Temples like Dalna served as a refuge for Jedi looking to meditate without distraction. These peaceful outposts were often a stop for students of the Force who needed time to recover from more traumatic events.

Unrest caused by the Nihil and very real concerns about how heavily the agricultural planet relied on a single cash crop had recently pushed the Dalnan government to join the Republic, but the people of Dalna remained cautious of their Jedi neighbors. When the Nihil began kidnapping Dalnan families, local authorities resisted assistance from the Order. One hundred fifty years of hard feelings after the Night of Sorrow were not easily set aside. It seems even the Jedi had a hard time reconciling what happened on Dalna in the past. The Jedi archives detailing the history of the system are locked behind security clearances held by only the highest-ranking members of the Order.

For many Jedi, a quiet agricultural planet with a population that fears space travel and distrusts Jedi might not be the most appealing posting, but the Dalna temple Jedi are not typical in many ways. The most experienced Jedi posted to Dalna was the Twi'lek Master Nyla Quinn. After many years of service, she welcomed the slower pace of life found on Dalna. Her calm demeanor was exactly what the Council needed for Dalna, as a more outgoing or inexperienced Jedi could risk spoiling the already strained relationship.

Another Jedi that could be counted on to keep a steady head was Yacek Sparkburn. Though he was a descendant of explorers and adventurers in the San Tekka clan, Yacek was not likely to seek out such trouble. Yacek enjoyed connecting to the Force through meditative hikes and was a better cook than a duelist. The temple was also home to a studious archivist, Lyssa Votz. A posting to Dalna, with its limited conflict, was the perfect assignment for Lyssa who was a scholar first and foremost. From a young age, she felt most at home among the archives. She wielded a blue saber so pale it is almost white, that is, if she remembers to bring her saber along at all. For Lyssa, a datapad was her more reliable companion, and she called upon it to answer any question with great zeal.

These Jedi of the Dalna temple were welcoming, if perhaps surprised, when more Jedi arrived to their quiet outpost in search for kidnapped children. Dalna, once the site of tragic frontier events, once again became central to the struggle between good and evil. The Nihil had secretly infiltrated the planet and calamity was sure to follow.

OPPOSITE Yacek Sparkburn, Nyla Quinn, and Lyssa Votz.

CHAPTER 7
THE FALL OF STARLIGHT

This is what hope is. It isn't pretending that nothing will go wrong if only we try hard enough. It's looking squarely at all the obstacles in the way—knowing the limits of our own power, and the possibility of failure—and moving ahead anyway. That is how we must proceed. With hope.

— STELLAN GIOS

CRISIS AT EIRAM AND ABROAD

Starlight Beacon existed to give hope to a corner of the galaxy that needed it most. For more than a year after its dedication, the Republic and Jedi worked in pursuit of that goal. Though we didn't realize it at the time, Starlight Beacon would serve its final days responding to a series of disasters across the Outer Rim. The Jedi, believing that the Nihil had been all but defeated, turned their attention to rescue efforts on Dalna and later Eiram.

Eiram had recently joined the Republic when it suffered a terrible cyclone. The planet relied on desalination plants to make its abundant salt water potable. The entire population and their crops depended upon these constructions to make the planet hospitable and, without them, would have lasted weeks at best.

With the deadly cyclone bearing down on Eiram's largest inhabited area, Starlight Beacon was towed from Dalna to the Eiram system so that the Republic and the Jedi could provide immediate assistance. As they had done so many times before, the Jedi joined minds through the Force, channeling all of its power to hold back the terrible waves. They achieved together what none of them could have done by themselves. The heroics earned the Jedi endless gratitude from the local population, and Queens Dima and Thandeka alike. Starlight remained in Eiram's orbit in preparation for the final repairs to the reconstructed desalination plants when further tragedies struck.

Across the galaxy, reports flowed in of Nihil attacks at disparate locations, but they all had just one thing in common: They were far apart. These attacks were seemingly without purpose but were no less disastrous for it. Jedi temples across the Outer Rim opened their doors to refugees, but the temple at Chespea fell under a direct targeted bombing attack that took the lives of all Jedi.

Starlight Beacon accepted refugees as well, opening its facilities to all who needed sanctuary from the influx of Nihil attacks. After all, the very purpose of the station was to serve as a beacon of hope to those who need it most. Starlight's medbays were filled with injured civilians who received the finest in medical care. The hangar bays were filled virtually to capacity by ships needing safe harbor and repairs. The Republic crews and Jedi alike worked to ensure no one was turned away in this great time of need. Like the rest of the station, even the holding cells were filled nearly to capacity by the mounting ranks of Nihil prisoners.

The Order scrambled to respond, leaving Starlight Beacon with fewer Jedi defenders than usual. With Avar Kriss leading the infiltration of a Nihil stronghold elsewhere in the galaxy, leaders speculated that these were the raiders' final desperate attacks, and would mark the end of their streak of terror.

We now believe these were diversionary strikes to cover for the true evil that was to come. Starlight Beacon itself was not safe, its Jedi were distracted, and perhaps something far more sinister was clouding the Order's judgment.

STUDENTS OF THE FORCE

When most beings envision a Jedi Knight, they likely conjure up some image of a lightsaber-wielding hero bounding into action in defense

OPPOSITE Jedi rescuers use the Force to hold back a tsunami on Eiram.

of the light, but we Jedi know that it takes much more than just warriors to serve the Force. Just as vital to our Order are the countless archivists and academics who ensure that the knowledge of the Jedi is preserved for generations to come.

The need for archivists rose in recent years as the Jedi expanded our role in the galaxy.

A permanent presence in so many systems led to an explosion of information. With every expedition, the Jedi returned to their temples with new discoveries, relics, and mysteries to be catalogued. The expertise of an archivist was vital to the proper classification and preservation of these finds.

In times of trouble, even an archivist is called to the blade. From Valo to the battle for Starlight Beacon, our Jedi academics proved to be worthy defenders of light, and as capable with a lightsaber as they were a datapad. The nature of recent battles meant that even an archivist could be in harm's way.

ESTALA MARU

The operation of Starlight Beacon was among the most complex jobs in the galaxy. It was a puzzle with many answers, moving pieces, and no final solution. It was the perfect job for Jedi Master Estala Maru.

Master Maru worked hand in hand with his Republic counterparts to ensure Starlight Beacon ran at peak efficiency. Day and night, he sat in the station's command hub, fueled by his natural passion for knowledge and a seemingly endless supply of mei-mei tea. The job required a vigorous attention to detail in order to manage Starlight's many systems and structures. He supervised the coming and going of nearly every vessel to the beacon's hangars and monitored communications in and around the station. He also oversaw the distribution of resources, as well as identifying available Jedi who could respond to the Nihil and Drengir emergencies.

Few would envy such a demanding role, but Master Maru was seemingly born for the job. His only regret was that the task took him away from his many other studies, including his particular interest in the Force Sculptors of the Old Republic. Maru's eye for detail undoubtedly gave him great appreciation for these ancient arts.

ORBALIN

Master OrbaLin was unlike any other Jedi in more ways than one. He regularly claimed to be the only Ugor ever to be accepted in the Jedi Order, a fact that he was exceptionally proud of. His species' unique biology required him to wear a containment suit that gave him a humanoid appearance, as his natural form was a cytoplasmic blob. This rare physique could be an advantage in combat and made Master OrbaLin virtually impervious to injuries that would stab or dismember other species.

Master OrbaLin was named a lead archivist assigned to Starlight Beacon in recognition for his expertise. He was legendary for his ability to lecture at length on nearly any subject, including any of the artifacts on display at Starlight's archive or the Jedi's exhibition at the Republic Fair. His deep appreciation for these items made him intensely protective when they fell under attack. During the tragedy on Valo, his knowledge of ancient technology allowed the Republic to send a distress

OPPOSITE Estala Maru coordinates Starlight Beacon and Jedi frontier operations from his observation station.

Burryaga faces rathtars on Starlight Beacon.

signal using an antique deep-space transmitter from the Jedi temple on Vrogas Vas, and he was one of the few Jedi to get the upper hand in a fight with the Nihil Tempest Runner Lourna Dee.

THE BATTLE FOR STARLIGHT BEACON

For more than a year, the Jedi used Starlight Beacon as their base of operations to combat the Nihil scourge. There were multiple attempts at sabotage, each discovered and deflected in short order by the beacon's Jedi defenders. Through quick reflexes and heightened sensitivities, the Force gave the Jedi the upper hand when saboteurs struck.

In the station's final days, something weakened the Jedi of Starlight Beacon's connection to the Force. A sense of dread fell upon many of them, similar feelings to those experienced on Grizal, but its source was unclear. This seemingly slight disruption allowed the Nihil to infiltrate deep into Starlight Beacon's core, where they expertly set upon their task to irreparably sabotage the very heart of the great station. When the Jedi felt the explosion, it was already too late.

The nature of the attack left the station nearly cut in two. The upper and lower halves were cut off by radiation spilling through conduits. In the hub of the station's upper half, Jedi led by Master Maru were unable to communicate with the Jedi of the lower half, who were being led by Master Gios.

In the station's spire, Master Maru poured himself into holding the station together to organize the Jedi response. The Jedi raced into action but soon realized that the greatest danger had not been caused by the explosion. Instead, the Jedi were being hunted by mysterious creatures that only attacked Force-users. Master Sskeer, having lost his connection to the Force due to Magrak Syndrome, was unfazed by the nameless creature's power. He elected to stay behind to combat the threat, allowing Keeve Trennis and Avar Kriss to escape. Master Torban Buck was trapped near the bio-gardens along with the young Padawans in his care, but the apprentices were saved by the arrival of Emerick Caphtor. While Caphtor escorted the young Jedi to safety aboard his ship, Torban Buck charged back into the fight against the mysterious foes.

Master Gios and the Jedi trapped in the lower portion of Starlight Beacon worked diligently to get refugee ships off the station, and allow docked vessels to escape. The escape pods were deactivated, so ships were packed to capacity with escaping passengers. Non-Jedi volunteers worked to restore power as the Jedi were puzzled over the mysterious enemies hiding somewhere in the station. Padawan Bell Zettifar showed great ingenuity when he blasted away the station's medical tower, releasing it and Starlight's wounded from the station's inevitable plummet.

Starlight Beacon was orbiting the planet Eiram in the days following its mercy mission. With its control systems virtually destroyed, the station was being pulled by the planet's gravity to its doom.

THE BEACON FALLS

Starlight Beacon could not be saved. The initial blast at the station's core severed communication and travel between each half of the station, but now Eiram's gravity was pulling the two apart.

OPPOSITE Starlight Beacon is destroyed while in Eiram's orbit.

In the lower portion of the beacon, Jedi Elzar Mann reactivated the station's positional thrusters to prevent that half from burning up in the planet's atmosphere. He had, at least temporarily, slowed its descent and adjusted its reentry angle to prevent a cataclysmic impact with the planet, but the upper portion had no such option.

The crown of Starlight Beacon fell toward reentry at a terminal velocity and could not withstand the extreme temperatures building up across its exterior. As it fell into Eiram's atmosphere, it burst into flames and shed molten fragments of itself. The Jedi who remained on board attempted to slow the station's fall, but even when united by Avar Kriss's Song of the Force, they could not stop the inevitable. Estala Maru stayed behind, conjuring every ounce of strength he had to hold the station together long enough for others to escape.

As the base of Starlight Beacon continued to plummet, a distress call reached nearby systems. Some believed the call for help to be a humorless prank and could not imagine the Republic's greatest Great Work was actually in grave danger. Thankfully, others readied flotillas of relief vessels and jumped to hyperspace. The relief effort came largely from civilians—those citizens of the galaxy who had long been protected by the Jedi came to our aid.

While many lives were spared, there was nothing that could save what remained of Starlight Beacon. The lower portion continued its collision course with one of Eiram's most populated cities, Barraza. Once most of the remaining ships and passengers had departed, a single Jedi selflessly stayed behind at the auxiliary controls of the station's positional thrusters. Just enough power remained to narrowly miss the city below where

thousands of survivors watched as the Republic's beacon of hope crashed into the sea.

STELLAN GIOS

The tragedies of recent years made Master Stellan Gios an icon of the Jedi Order. Stellan was as if the personification of a classic Jedi jumped from the holos and into real life. Looking back on his perfectly archetypal path from youngling to Master, it was as if achieving greatness was always his destiny.

Since he was a youngling, Stellan Gios embraced the traditions and rules of our Order. Whereas his peer Elzar Mann was a tinkerer, Gios rarely veered from convention or the wisdom of his master, Rana Kant. While not particularly great with animals nor droids, he was quick to rise through the ranks and named a member of the Jedi Council in the wake of his former master's death. Stellan Gios saw the Force as a constellation of stars, each light representing a single life. He himself was a rising star among the Jedi Order, but it was the tragedy at Valo that propelled him into the public eye.

Master Gios was the leading Jedi representative for the opening ceremonies of the Republic Fair, where he was tasked with accompanying Chancellor Lina Soh and her honored guest, the Togruta regasa Elarec Yovet. When the Nihil struck on the fair's second day, he personally oversaw their escape to safety. Though he defended them from numerous assaults, Nihil bombs nearly took the chancellor's life during the battle's waning phase. As the Nihil escaped across the galaxy, the image of Stellan Gios cradling the gravely injured chancellor was broadcast across the holonet, instantly making him an icon of the tragedy.

As Avar Kriss, marshal of Starlight Beacon, took to hunting the Nihil threat, Master Gios stepped in as the leader of the station out of necessity. No one predicted that he would be there to see the station through its final days. As Stellan oversaw the arrival of refugees from the most recent wave of attacks, the Nihil infiltrated Starlight Beacon with agents who avoided detection long enough to cause a cataclysmic explosion that broke the station in two.

As he worked from a makeshift command center in the lower half of the station, Master Stellan Gios's levelheaded leadership saved many lives while Starlight Beacon fell into Eiram's orbit below. The station was on a course to crash into a heavily populated city, endangering thousands of lives on Eiram. Master Stellan personally took manual control of the station's thrusters to safely guide it away from the city. A summary of those final moments provided by his droid, JJ-5145, suggests that Master Gios might have had time to abandon the controls for the safety of an escape pod, but chose to remain at his station to ensure that Starlight reached the safest point of impact. He knowingly sacrificed his own life to save just a few others.

Memorials to Starlight Beacon honor that day when the light of the Republic on the frontier went dark. But we Jedi know that the brightest star at Eiram was not a space station: It was the radiant light of Master Stellan Gios, which burned so luminously until the very end.

ABOVE Stellan Gios prevents the falling space station from crashing into a city, at the cost of his own life.

THE CORELLIAN PLOT

For most of our struggle against the Nihil, their savagery was concentrated in the galaxy's Outer Rim. Many in the Republic continued to view the Nihil threat as a frontier problem and believed that they would never stray from their usual hunting grounds. Those illusions were shattered when the Jedi discovered a Nihil plot on the Core World of Corellia.

Corellia is one of the Republic's premiere shipbuilding worlds. Its docks famously construct some of the finest, fastest, and largest vessels that travel the galaxy. The shipyards construct YT-series freighters, Republic Longbeams, and the modern MPO-1400 *Purrgil*-class star cruisers destined for the Chandrila Star Line's luxury tours. The Nihil, led by Krix Kamerat, formulated a plot to infiltrate and destabilize the local bureaucracy, but terror on Corellia was just part of their ultimate goal.

The Jedi now know the plot was not a localized attempt at subversion. Instead, the Nihil intended to commandeer a fleet of Corellian ships and reposition them to the ill-fated Starlight Beacon to terrorize the rescue effort. It was to be the final phase of their vicious attack on the Republic's Great Work.

The plot was ultimately foiled by a team of Jedi sent to respond to the reports of Nihil activity. Led by Masters Kantam Sy and Cohmac Vitus, the outnumbered Jedi and their Corellian allies waged a valiant defense to prevent the Nihil from carrying out their plans. The arrival of Master Yoda was a pivotal turning point in the battle and ultimately led to a hard-fought victory. Reath Silas earned his elevation to knighthood, but there was little joy to be had in the moment.

In the wake of the Corellian battle, the Jedi were struck as they felt the loss of Starlight Beacon from across the galaxy. The ordeal at the docks, the loss of Starlight, and the mounting pressure of battles past led Master Cohmac to declare that he was leaving the Jedi Order. Corellia itself still reels from the attack. The corruption ran so deeply that the planet has become engulfed in a civil war.

KANTAM SY

Long before they were elevated to the rank of Jedi Master, Kantam Sy was the Padawan of Master Yoda, one of the Order's most renowned teachers. The duo's paths would diverge and converge

OPPOSITE Kantam Sy faces off against Nihil raiders.

throughout Sy's life, as they took a unique route to knighthood. Shortly before Sy was to be knighted, they stepped away from their Jedi training for a personal journey of self-reflection and discovery. In his great wisdom, Master Yoda allowed such an interlude, allowing the Force to guide young Sy to their destiny. For at the end of their time away, Kantam Sy rescued a youngling in need, only to realize that she had exceptional Force abilities. That youngling was Lula Talisola, who later became Master Sy's own apprentice.

Master Sy served with Yoda as an instructor on the *Star Hopper*, shepherding the extraordinary group of Padawans through a most difficult time in galactic history. They served as both a wise teacher and staunch defender across so many battles, defending the Republic and their Padawans from Quantxi to Corellia.

REEVALUATING OUR ADVERSARIES

After more than a year of conflict with the Nihil, the fall of Starlight is a moment that forces us to pause and reflect upon those who have put the Jedi on the defensive. It was easy to underestimate the Nihil, believing them to be a mere band of mercenaries whose only motivation was plunder and chaos. For lower-ranking members of the Nihil, that seems to be true. But clearly there is something larger at play, with someone more sophisticated pulling the strings.

The Jedi and Republic have long known that the leader of the Nihil is their Eye. We believed, incorrectly and for far too long, that the Eye of the Nihil was the ruthless Twi'lek, Lourna Dee. We poured our resources into finding her in hopes that her capture would bring this nightmare to an end,

but time and again she slipped from our grasp. Only now have we learned that Lourna Dee is only a Tempest Runner, a high-ranking commander and dangerous in her own right, but not the ultimate leader of the Nihil we sought. It was an unprecedented intelligence failure for which we ultimately paid a heavy price.

Alarmingly, we now understand that there is a Nihil spy working in Republic Chancellor Lina Soh's inner circle. Using their access to the highest-ranking politicians in the government, they have fed the Nihil vital information and allowed the most senior Nihil leadership to stay one step ahead of our justice.

The true Eye of the Nihil has revealed himself—a mysterious and soft spoken man, Marchion Ro. Little is known about Ro or his motivations, but the fact that he hid himself from us for so long suggests that he is a calculating and patient challenger to the Republic. He has taken credit for everything the Nihil have done, from the *Legacy Run* disaster to the fall of Starlight Beacon. He commands the Tempests, Storms, and Strikes that comprise the Nihil fleet. He is behind the kidnapping plots, temple attacks, and merciless raids that threaten life in the Outer Rim. He has halted progress in the Outer Rim and caused some to question our very place so far from the galactic core. And worst of all for the Jedi, he is in command of a most deadly and debilitating weapon.

It is becoming clear now that Ro is somehow connected to the nameless, mysterious creatures we encountered on Grizal, Xais, and during the fall of Starlight—the beasts responsible for the deaths of far too many Jedi. Emerick Caphtor's investigation uncovered a well-connected Nihil doctor attempting to sell one of these living weapons on the black

market. The plot was foiled, but not in time to prevent the tragedy at the Beacon.

The Jedi will not underestimate the Nihil any longer. Marchion Ro is one of the greatest enemies to light and life we have ever faced.

THE JEDI AT BEACON'S END

The galaxy at large is still reeling from the loss of Starlight Beacon. It's still hard to believe that such a monumental achievement is simply gone. Harder yet is the realization that the lights of the Jedi were extinguished during the attack.

The list of Jedi confirmed lost on Starlight Beacon continues to grow. Among the names of heroes taken are Master Stellan Gios, who gave his life to save those citizens of Eiram. Master Estala Maru held the station together until the very end, and his sacrifice allowed countless passengers to escape.

We lost many Jedi to the same mysterious creatures that struck Loden Greatstorm on Grizal. Nib Assek, Regald Coll, Nooranbakarakana, and Orla Jareni were all killed during their encounters with this nameless, faceless enemy. We still don't understand why some were turned to husks and others could escape, but we honor those who stayed behind to combat the threats. Jedi Masters Sskeer and Torban Buck both charged toward the enemy and have not been seen since. Thanks to Master Buck's sacrifice, many young Padawans were able to evacuate under the care of the newly knighted Qort.

The fate of other Padawans remains uncertain. Lula Talisola and Farzala Tarabal are missing. Farzala's former master, Obratuk Glii, has also not been seen since the attack. The archivist OrbaLin and the engineer Monshi had attempted to escape aboard the *Ataraxia*, but the ship and its crew have not been recovered.

The Wookiee Padawan Burryaga was last seen fighting rathtars who had escaped their enclosures in Starlight's docking bay. His bravery in battle allowed many survivors to escape through the lower station's cargo bay, but it is unclear if he could have survived the fight against those vicious creatures. Padawan Bell Zettifar has committed to finding his friend, should the Wookiee have miraculously survived.

Though they are reeling from the loss of their friend Stellan Gios, Masters Avar Kriss and Elzar Mann escaped the station with their lives. Keeve Trennis has emerged stronger and more confident than before the attack, while her friends Ceret and Terec have emerged from their hibernation state. These Jedi have all faced unspeakable hardship over the past year, but their experiences combating the galaxy's threats—including the Nihil and the nameless creatures—will be invaluable as the Jedi consider our next moves.

Emerick Caphtor's investigation into the mysterious Force-sensitive creatures led him to Starlight Beacon during the attack and allowed him to witness the beings for himself. Study of specimens taken from the disaster scene are being analyzed by the Order's finest scientists, archivists, and historians. Though it has been hard-earned, we have more understanding than ever before of the dangers before us.

Jedi among those confirmed dead or missing after the fall of Starlight. Background, left to right: Obratuk Glii, Nooranbakarakana, OrbaLin, Estala Maru, Stellan Gios, Torban Buck, Burryaga, and Regald Coll Foreground, left to right: Sskeer, Orla Jareni, Monshi, Lula Talisola, Farzala Tarabal, and Nib Assek.

AFTERWORD

The Jedi ventured into the Outer Rim believing we could help usher in an age of prosperity by sharing the light of the Force in dark corners of the galaxy. For a time, we achieved that goal. Billions of lives at Hetzal were saved by Jedi rescuers. New systems joined the Republic, and through that partnership, we saved countless lives from natural and unnatural disasters. Starlight Beacon provided aid and safe harbor to thousands, and we have learned much about the galaxy along the way.

The unintended consequence of our intervention into the Outer Rim was that we have awakened enemies—both new and old—who threaten our Order in ways that we have not seen in generations. More Jedi died in this past year than in the previous three decades combined. In the wake of Starlight Beacon's fall, dozens of Jedi are unaccounted for and a mysterious foe that targets Jedi remains at large.

The High Council has recalled all Jedi back to the Grand Temple on Coruscant, including myself. The nameless, faceless beasts that weakened or killed so many are simply too dangerous to the Jedi for us to remain scattered across the galaxy. At Master Yoda's urging, we must regather our strength and find a way to defend ourselves from this threat. For as long as we cannot combat this danger, we cannot protect others from the Nihil marauders.

Our understanding of the Nihil has changed considerably in recent weeks. A man named Marchion Ro revealed himself as the true Eye of the Nihil and declared a corner of the galaxy his territory. Ten sectors were sealed away behind a barrier that prevents hyperspace jumps into the Exclusion Zone. Communications in and out of this region have failed, and the Nihil have begun to expand their presence in the Outer Rim. Wherever they rule, horrific brutality follows.

As I write these words, the Jedi have formed a special council to orchestrate our response. We have allies behind the enemy lines and still others who are willing to break the blockade. Their bravery inspires us in this time where we must use caution. Even with our very connection to the Force in doubt, there are many of us Jedi who remain committed to returning to the frontier so that we may once again spread light when the galaxy needs it most.

For light and life!

The Force surrounds us.

The Force dwells in us.

The Force flows through us.

The Force protects us.

The Force is strong.

For the Force is light.

INSIGHT
EDITIONS

PO Box 3088
San Rafael, CA 94912
www.insighteditions.com

Find us on Facebook: www.facebook.com/InsightEditions

Follow us on Twitter: @insighteditions

ISBN (Trade): 978-1-64722-644-2
ISBN (Collector's Edition): 979-8-88663-035-0

Publisher: Raoul Goff
VP of Licensing and Partnerships: Vanessa Lopez
VP of Creative: Chrissy Kwasnik
VP of Manufacturing: Alix Nicholaeff
VP, Editorial Director: Vicki Jaeger
Art Director: Stuart Smith
Editor: Harrison Tunggal
Editorial Assistants: Grace Orriss and Emma Merwin
Managing Editor: Maria Spano
Senior Production Managers: Greg Steffen & Joshua Smith
Senior Production Manager, Subsidiary Rights: Lina s Palma-Temena

For Lucasfilm
Editor: Jennifer Pooley
Senior Editor: Brett Rector
Creative Director: Michael Siglain
Art Director: Troy Alders
Story Group: Leland Chee, Pablo Hidalgo, and Kate Izquierdo
Creative Art Manager: Phil Szostak
Asset Management: Elinor De La Torre and Sarah Williams

Written by Cole Horton
Illustrated by Yihyoung Li
Additional color by Alberto Buscicchio
Lightsaber insert art on page 113 by Łukasz Liszko

ROOTS of PEACE   REPLANTED PAPER

Insight Editions, in association with Roots of Peace, will plant two trees for each tree used in the manufacturing of this book. Roots of Peace is an internationally renowned humanitarian organization dedicated to eradicating land mines worldwide and converting war-torn lands into productive farms and wildlife habitats. Roots of Peace will plant two million fruit and nut trees in Afghanistan and provide farmers there with the skills and support necessary for sustainable land use.

Manufactured in China by Insight Editions

10 9 8 7 6 5 4 3 2 1